99 Days

AnnaLisa Grant

99 Days
Copyright © 2016 by AnnaLisa Grant
All rights reserved
ISBN-13: 978-1535253024
ISBN-10: 1535253029

Cover art Marisa Shor at Cover Me, Darling

For more information, visit:
www.AnnaLisaGrant.com
Facebook.com/AuthorAnnalisaGrant

This book is a work of fiction. The names, characters, places and incidents are products of the writer's imagination or have been used fictitiously and are not to be construed as real. Any resemblance to person, living or dead, actual events, locales or organizations is entirely coincidental.

Dedication

For the survivors of atrocities no one should ever endure.
Your strength and tenacity inspire me beyond measure.

Day 99

Water dripped from my eyelashes as I stared at the whirlpool forming at the drain of the shower. It was the color of shit, fitting since that's what I felt like. Dirt caked my feet, creating black lines under my toenails. Blood, mud, and the untraceable amounts of dried semen left on me washed away, revealing my peach colored skin. Soon my body would be clean, and I'd look as though nothing had ever happened to me. I'd look like a normal eighteen-year-old girl. I would never be normal, though. I used to be, before the day I was knocked unconscious and tossed into the bed of a pickup truck like a bag of feed. But there I was, used, tainted, and feeling very *not* normal, preparing to go back to the life I used to have.

"Caroline?" a woman's sweet voice called through the bathroom door. "Do you need anything?"

"No. I'm fine, thank you," I called back.

The water finally flowed crystal clear. After nearly scrubbing off a layer of skin, I'd scoured my body as clean as I could get it. No more dirt, no more remnants of him soiled me. I turned the shower dial all the way to the left, letting the almost scalding pellets of water pound away the tension in my neck. The soap had gotten me clean, but the heat would sanitize me. And that's what I needed. To be sanitized.

I turned the shower off and wrapped a towel around my body. Eyeing the scrubs Nurse MaryKay gave me, I recalled her apology for underwear that looked like an adult diaper. Going "commando" was fine with me. As gentle as they tried to be during the extensive gynecological exam, fresh discomfort seeped in. I had done a good job of disconnecting myself from everything he did to me but, as I lay on the exam table staring blankly at the ceiling, the wall I had built began to crumble. The only relief that exam brought was a negative pregnancy test. The idea of carrying that monster's baby made me want to die. I had only a faint period three weeks after I had been taken, and nothing since. But the doctor assured me that the level of stress I was under was enough to make me miss my period.

I wiped the foggy mirror with my arm. My lip had split and the whole left side of my face bruised around the stitches in my cheek. My whole body seemed sore to the touch, but the pain subsided with the meds MaryKay had given me.

Dressed, with my hair combed and my teeth brushed, I sat down on the closed lid of the toilet. He was out there. I knew it. I wanted to him to be there. He was my father, but I didn't know what I would feel when he first saw me. Would I look different? Would he even be able to look at me?

A light knock at the door preceded his voice.

"Caroline?" he said. His tentative voice may have even trembled as my name left his lips.

I took a deep breath and winced. The nurse said my side would ache for a while. I hadn't broken anything, but my body got bruised up pretty bad from my fall into the gully.

"Give it time," she said. "All things heal with time."

Sure they do.

My nervous, white-knuckled hand gripped the doorknob and twisted. I pulled slowly and waited for my father's face to appear.

He didn't look any different. I don't know why I thought he might. It had been over three months since I'd seen him. Still 6'2" with dark brown hair and tanned skin from life on the farm, my father had movie star quality looks.

"Hi, Dad," I said, just above a whisper.

"Hi, Caroline," he said back. He opened his arms, and I moved faster into them than I had since being a little girl. His strong arms held me close to the comforting warmth of his body.

"Are you ... okay?" he asked.

I nodded my lie against his chest. I might not ever be okay.

"How's Mom?" I asked him. I knew she wouldn't be able to come. The hospital was an hour from where the trucker picked me up, and still an hour and a half from my hometown of Pinewood.

"Don't worry about your mom. Focus on getting rest and letting the doctors make sure you're okay." His breath wisped across the top of my head as he spoke. "You'll see her when you get out of here."

"We've completed our part," MaryKay interrupted. "But the police need to ask her a few questions."

"Um ... okay," I said.

MaryKay smiled politely and left the room. She returned less than a minute later with two police officers in full uniform, one female and one male.

"Hi, Caroline. I'm Officer Moore, and this is Officer Day with the Pinewood Police Department. I'm sure you're ready to get some rest, but we have a few questions to ask you about what happened," the female officer said.

Dad immediately looked down. The thought of hearing about what I had endured made him uncomfortable. I couldn't say I was excited about it either.

"I'll leave you ..." he began. He took three steps toward the door before Officer Day spoke up.

"We have all the *other* details from the doctor's report, Mr. Patterson. We just need Caroline to fill in some of the other information for our investigation."

"Oh. All right." Dad locked his knees and shoved his hands in his pockets. His signature move when he didn't know what to say or do.

"You were picked up on Saw Mill Road in Pollack County," Officer Moore began.

"I guess that's right," I said.

"Can you tell us anything about the direction from which you came? Had you just come from the woods when the trucker found you, or had you walked a bit first?"

"Um ... I came through the woods and walked for a while. Maybe a mile or two."

"Did you know the man who held you?" Office Day asked. "Had you seen him before?"

"No. I was waiting to have lunch with my cousin at the diner in town. He said he needed a jump but didn't have any jumper cables and asked if I could help," I told them.

"Did he ever tell you his name?" Office Moore asked.

"I only got his first name. Mud."

I found the side of the bed and sat down. My legs were weak, and answering their questions left me mentally drained.

"You're doing really well, Caroline," Officer Moore said, seeing my growing weariness.

"How many more of these questions does she need to answer? She's been through enough and needs to rest." My father took his hands out of his pockets and closed the distance between him and the officers. He didn't always play the intimidation card, but when he did, it played well.

"Just a few more, Mr. Patterson. I know this is difficult, but it's important to get as much information from your daughter while things are still fresh. The sooner we have what we need, the sooner we can fully investigate her kidnapping and get the bastard who did this." The way Officer Day looked at my father, I wondered if he had kids of his own. He seemed to understand what Dad was going through.

"Were you in a house?" Officer Moore continued her questioning. "Was it on a busy street or a more rural area? Did you see any other houses? Neighbors?"

I lowered my head and swallowed hard. Thinking about that place, about Mud ... It was hard to breathe.

"A house," I said. "A small house in the middle of the woods."

"Do you remember what it looked like?" Office Day asked, his voice growing more assertive. He dug for information I couldn't give him.

"No."

"There are countless houses in the woods out there," Officer Moore said. "Isn't there any detail you can tell us? You were there for three months—"

"99 days," my father interrupted, correcting her. "She was gone for 99 days." My heart ached knowing he and Mom counted each one of those days.

"I never saw the outside of the house. I was blindfolded when I got there, and when I ran, I didn't look back." I pulled the rest of my body onto the bed, tucked my legs under the covers, and lay my head on the pillow.

"Okay, that's enough. You asked your questions. She needs to rest," my father insisted.

Officer Moore stepped closer to the bed and put her hand on my shoulder. "You did really well, Caroline. We'll come back later, after you've had time to rest. You're very brave."

Dad ushered the officers out into the hall and closed the door behind them, leaving me alone.

Brave. If I were brave, I would have taken Owen with me when I escaped.

Day 1

The screen door flew open and crashed closed.

"Hey, Uncle Andrew!" my cousin Peter said as he charged into the living room. He was two years older than me, full of life, and didn't do anything with less than an enthusiastic attitude. Tall with brown hair and eyes, he looked just like all the Patterson men. That gene pool only knew how to make one model, and I'm the female version. "We've got two cap bolt pistols on the fritz. I called Sonny down at the feed store, and he said he could fix 'em, but I gotta take 'em today."

"Well then you better get down there," Dad told him. "And I better get back out to the barn. I think Maribelle is going to have her calf any day now." He kissed Mom on the cheek and me on the head and patted Peter on the back as he left.

"I wish he wouldn't name them," I said with a sigh.

"Why? It's not like we're killin' the ones we name," Peter offered.

"Yeah, but we're going to raise and kill their babies. It's just weird," I countered. "You want a drink for the road, Pete?"

"Sure! Thanks, Care."

"Why don't you go with him?" Mom suggested.

I tried to tell her I couldn't leave her because she was always so worn out after chemo, and that I needed to stay to help her, but she held her hand up and stopped me before I uttered a single word.

"I'm just going to sleep for the next few hours. There's no use in you hanging around here. It's a gorgeous day. Get out in the truck and enjoy the drive into town."

I twisted my mouth in contemplation.

"Are you sure?" Mom's raised eyebrows told me I'd better not push back too hard. "Yes, ma'am." I kissed her on the cheek and moved toward the kitchen. "I'll get you a glass of water before I leave. Is there anything you want while I'm in town?"

"I can't think of anything, but I'll text you if I change my mind," she said with a victorious smile.

The screen door slammed behind me. I climbed inside the cab of Peter's truck and we drove to the slaughter building.

"So what's wrong with the cap bolt pistols? I thought Dad got new ones when he built the holding pen," I asked.

Dad generally resisted anything modern when it came to the farm, and only two years ago he built a facility with a moveable box chute to expedite the humane killing of cattle. He still trained new guys to use a .22 caliber rifle to take out the beef cattle, though. He was old school like that. Hell, he even made me learn how to use the rifle before he would let me near a cap bolt gun.

"It's the old ones that're getting stuck when the pin comes out. Makes it messy when you try to pull the sucker out of the poor beast's head." Peter made a jerking motion with his head. I punched him in the arm and scrunched my face.

"Ew!"

"Hey! Those new guns Uncle Andrew got that hang over the box chute are awesome. If it were up to me, I'd get rid of these old ones and keep us 100% in the 21st Century."

We rolled up to the slaughter building and Peter jumped out. He was back in less than a minute with the pistols that needed fixing and we were on the main road in two.

With the windows down, I pulled my hair back and let the wind blow in my face. I loved living in what seemed like the middle of nowhere. I loved how tall stalks of corn stood at attention and the way fields of wheat swayed with the wind. I even loved the way it smelled, that blend of fresh air and fresh cow manure.

The closest schools were almost an hour away, and Mom didn't see the point in that kind of travel time. So she homeschooled me, and I enjoyed a perfect country life on the farm. I loved everything about my life … except the fact that my mom had cancer and was readying herself to die.

"Sorry about barging in on you guys earlier," Peter said loudly over the howl of the wind.

"It's okay," I replied.

He pressed his lips together like he was trying to decide if he should ask me what was on his mind. "Is Aunt Mary gonna be okay?" he finally asked.

"That depends on your definition of okay. The mass isn't shrinking, but the doc wants to try a new treatment on her, so we've at least got that, for now," I told him.

"I'm sorry," he said. He put his hand on my shoulder and nudged it. "Listen, your mom is going to nap for a while. We'll drop off the pistols and go over to Anderson's for a late lunch. My treat!"

"That'd be awesome." I smiled.

"Hope Andy's workin'. God, I love razzing that guy about his name." Peter let out a loud guffaw. "Pft! Andy Anderson!"

"Dude! Your name is Peter Patterson. Like that's much better!" I laughed.

"Shut up!" Peter scowled and then laughed.

We walked through the 100-year-old door to Renfrow's Feed and Hardware Store. The clanging bell above the door startled me every time. The floors creaked with every step, and you had to watch your balance because they sloped in random places. Old Man Renfrow swore he'd never change a thing about his grandfather's store, and he never did. He unapologetically ordered the same products from the same catalog for as long as his predecessors had. Now that his son had taken over, though, things were starting to look a little more modern.

"Hey Sonny!" Peter called out. Sonny appeared from the back room with a grin the size of Texas.

"Hey, Peter! I didn't know you were bringin' Caroline with you! What a treat! Good to see you, darlin'!" Sonny was built like a linebacker and had movie star good looks. He blushed every time I told him so.

"Hey, Sonny." I waved as I approached the counter. "I heard you're going to fix my father's old-school toys!"

"I'm gonna try!" he laughed. "C'mon back! I gotta show you this new line of garden tools I'm getting for the store! Got the online catalog pulled up right now!"

"Ooooh! Online catalog! Progressive!" I snorted. "I'm gonna pass and head over to Anderson's if that's cool with you, Peter."

"That's cool," he replied. "Order me a Cherry Coke, will ya? I'll be over in a few minutes."

Outside, I passed the huge planters the local garden club had placed in memory of their president after she passed the year before. They were filled with purple and white impatiens, her favorite. I crossed at the light and headed straight into Anderson's Diner. Like most of the businesses in Pinewood, it had been family owned and operated since time began in our small town.

I wouldn't say everyone knew everyone, but we were a friendly, country community. We gathered in town on the 4th of July to watch the Haymitches set off fireworks from their farm. And no one dared miss the tree lighting in the center of town at Christmas.

I took a seat at a booth by the window and perused the menu while I waited for Peter. It was after three and practically a ghost town with just a few old timers at the counter having their requisite afternoon cup of coffee. I smiled at how cute they were. Before I turned my attention back to the menu, I extended my smile to the man sitting across from me four booths away. A good-looking guy with light brown hair, I guessed him to be about my dad's age, early 40's. He returned the smile and nodded politely before he took the last bites of his lunch. Several minutes went by and, as I decided on the patty melt, he walked past me and out the door.

"Hey, Caroline! What brings you into town this time of day?" Meg, the lead waitress at Anderson's said as she approached me. She said that when she married the owner, Paul, she married the diner. She stood at the ready with her pen and pad in hand.

"Hey, Meg," I said back. "Peter had to bring some cap bolt pistols to Sonny to fix, so we're going to have a late lunch. Mom had a doctor's appointment today, and I missed it earlier."

"How is she, honey?" Meg asked. She dropped her hands to her waist and tilted her head in concern.

"She's as well as can be expected. Cancer sucks and the treatment itself sucks the life out of you in the process. But we're all gettin' by."

"Well you tell her that she is in my prayers every night, okay?" Meg softened her voice and tilted her head to the other side. "You know what you want?"

"I'll hold off on ordering food until Peter gets here, but can you bring me a Sprite and him a Cherry Coke?" I asked.

"Got it, honey. Let me know if you need anything else before he gets here!"

Meg walked into the kitchen. I watched her through the window whispering something to Paul, who was working the grill. He looked up at me and smiled compassionately.

I looked outside for Peter. He was taking forever and I was getting hungrier by the minute. I didn't see Peter, but I did see the man who had been eating across from me only a few minutes before. He'd lifted the hood on his dark green truck, and then walked around to the bed of the vehicle. He caught my eye as he came back to the driver's door and continued until he walked through the door of the diner again.

"Excuse me, miss?" the man said politely. "My truck won't start. I don't suppose you've got a set of jumper cables. I'll be damned if I didn't forget to put them back in after I cleaned my truck out!" He laughed, a little embarrassed.

"We've all been there!" I chuckled. "I think my cousin has some in his truck, but it's across the street at Renfrow's. If you want, we can go see."

"That'd be great. Thanks! I'll meet you out there."

I stood up from the booth as Meg returned with our sodas.

"I'll be right back, Meg. I'm going to see if Peter has any jumper cables in his car for that guy." I pointed to the man, as he walked to his truck.

"Sure thing, honey," she replied.

I grabbed my phone and walked out the door, texting Peter that I was on my way and asked about the cables. He still hadn't replied to my last text. It had been long enough that I expected to see him walking down the sidewalk, but he wasn't there. I reached the bed of the man's truck, where he waited for me next to the lowered tailgate. The black vinyl cover was secured over the bed, creating an ominous cave.

"It's the blue one, right over there," I said to him. I pointed across the street at Peter's truck. Then I felt a sharp blow to my head, and everything went dark.

When I came to, I had a massive headache. My eyes tried to adjust in the pitch dark. My ankles were tied together, as were my hands. My heart began a panicked pace. I rolled involuntarily and realized I was moving.

I lay on my back, my foggy brain adding things up: the man from the diner lured me outside, hit me with something, and shoved me in the bed of his truck.

Oh my God.

I tried pulling my wrists apart, but they wouldn't budge. There was no give in the rope, which told me it wasn't nylon but natural fiber. The way it scratched around my wrist was also a dead giveaway. I felt around the ropes with my mouth and located the knot. I started biting and pulling at it with my teeth, spitting out the musty tasting fibers as I gnawed. It wouldn't move an inch. It was like it was double knotted and then double knotted again.

I reached above and in front of me as much as I could, hoping to find a tool of some kind that would help me. Swatting at air and then running my hands along the grooves of the truck bed, I found nothing. I rolled to the other side of the truck and did the same. Still nothing. I kicked my legs like a mermaid on dry land in hopes of finding anything useful. My foot found something small and flimsy, so I bent my body and wormed my way to the tailgate. Reaching my hands around the corner by the tailgate I found what had looped around my foot: jumper cables.

Wait! The tailgate! God, please let me be able to open the tailgate from in here!

I slid my hand along the top edge of the tailgate and felt nothing but smooth metal. I squirmed my body back around and tried kicking it open. I couldn't get enough force in my legs to feel like I did anything to it.

Oh, my God! Oh, my God! Oh, my God! Okay. It's going to be okay. Meg saw the guy, and I told her I was going to help him. Surely she'll be able to describe him to the police. And maybe Peter was on his way out of Renfrow's and saw the truck. Maybe Peter is following us right now and the cops are on their way.

The truck stopped and so did my heart. I shoved my body as far away from the tailgate as possible, as if that would make him change his mind about whatever he had planned for me. The tailgate dropped and sunlight flooded in. I looked around the bed and saw it truly was empty except for the jumper cables, which I was pretty sure he left in there to taunt me.

"Give me your legs," he demanded.

"NO!" I shouted at him.

"I'll come in there and get you, and that won't be pretty. So give me your goddamn legs!" The pleasantness of his voice and demeanor from the diner had vanished, and the scary harshness of his true self was left.

Maybe if I cooperated it'd be over quickly. I just had to survive. No matter what happened, I had to survive.

Be brave. Even when you're scared, be brave.

I inched my way toward the tailgate. His hands reached in and pulled my body halfway out. I couldn't see past his torso to have even a clue of where he had taken me. Not that it would have made a difference. I didn't know how long I had been out. Had we driven for hours, or was I thirty minutes up the road, so close to home, yet so far away?

"Close your eyes," he instructed.

"Why?"

"I said, close your fucking eyes! And if you make a sound, you'll regret it." He waited three seconds and then pulled the rest of my body out of the truck bed. My shirt slid up and the heat of the metal on my skin made me wince. He jerked my body upright, my feet landing solidly on the ground. Again I hoped if I cooperated he might go easy on me, so I closed my eyes … and my mouth.

When I landed on the ground, the rustle of leaves and the snapping of twigs under my feet told me we were in the woods. No sounds or smells indicated any animals nearby at all. We weren't in animal farm country. Another scent lingered in the air, but I couldn't put my finger on it.

He tied something around my eyes and flung me over his shoulder like a sack of feed. He was strong. I weighed 130 pounds, but he lifted me like a 50-pound bag of feed. He walked for a solid minute before stopping. Was he limping or was the ground uneven? I heard the flick of a switchblade and an involuntary yelp escaped my lips. Tears began to soak my blindfold.

"Shut it! I'm cuttin' the ropes off your feet," he said. That settled me only slightly. "I'm going to put you down. If you try to run, I will beat your ass to the ground."

He put me down and my back slammed against something. A tree? A wall?

With my eyes incapacitated, my hearing seemed supercharged. He jerked open a door that had the same manufactured plastic-against-metal sound the doors to the holding pen and slaughter buildings on the farm did. His fingers wrapped tightly around my bicep as he pulled me behind him. I had no sense of direction, banging against the narrow hall like a pinball. The floor bounced slightly and felt hollow under my feet. My shoulder slammed into the doorframe as we entered a room. He got in front of me and put his hands on my shoulders, guiding me back until my legs hit something.

"Sit down," he barked.

I didn't obey fast enough so he pushed me down. It was a bed. My body appreciated the softness of it after having knocking around the bed of his truck, but the reality of what was about to happen outweighed everything.

"Please. You don't have to do this," I pleaded. "If you let me go, I promise I won't tell anyone anything. Please! My mom is sick!"

"You talk too much. And I didn't bring you here for no talkin'," he said.

His words hit me hard because I knew exactly what he meant.

"I'm gonna take this blindfold off. Don't try anything."

I held my breath as his warm hands moved near my face. They smelled like oil and dirt, the way my father would smell after working on his car. He lifted the blindfold off my face and shoved it in his back pocket. I looked up at him and didn't think him good-looking any longer. I saw only a monster standing in front of me.

"Please!" I began to beg again, and he raised his hand like he was going to hit me. I cowered and put my still-bound hands up in defense.

"That's right," he said, dropping his hand to his side. "Let's keep it that way. Now, you sit tight. I'll be right back."

He left the room and closed the door behind him. The next thing I heard was the squeak of a latch flipping, its tap against the door, and the click of a padlock. I counted to ten and slowly lifted myself off the bed and moved to the door. The knob turned, but the door wouldn't move.

I turned around and surveyed my surroundings. A double bed with a metal headboard, neatly made up with light blue bedding, had been pushed into a corner of the stark white bedroom. The matching comforter had been turned down, and a small nightstand sat next to it, empty. A slender door revealed a small closet. There were two narrow windows at the top of one wall. Too high to reach, and too small to climb through.

Behind another door, a small bathroom big enough for just a stall shower, toilet, and a tiny, wall-mounted sink. No mirror hung above it.

There was nothing in the place I could use as a weapon of self-defense. What was I going to do?

Footsteps stampeded down the hallway, getting louder as they reached the bedroom door. I took my place back on the bed where the man had left me and waited for my fate. When the door opened, my kidnapper stood there, but he wasn't alone. He brought a friend.

"Look, Owen!" my captor said. "I brought you a gift!"

Owen looked at me with confusion, his brows knitted together and eyes darting between my abductor and me. I understood what the man meant, but it was somehow lost on Owen.

"What do you mean she's a gift, Mud?" Owen asked.

Mud? His name was Mud? Of course this dirt bag would have such a fitting name.

Owen's voice was slow and concentrated, like pronouncing each word was difficult. He looked from me to the man, apparently struggling to understand what Mud meant. I could see he had developmental challenges and the *generosity* of Mud's gift to him disgusted me.

"You've been doin' real good at studying those movies, so I figured it was time for you to graduate to the real thing," Mud told him. "Time for you to become a real man!"

My stomach turned and I scooted into the corner, pulling my knees to my chest. He brought me there so his friend could learn how to have sex? This guy was an asshole on so many levels. No. Not an asshole. That word was too kind. He was a monster. Pure evil. I had to get out of there, but I couldn't see how.

"I don't know, Mud," Owen said. "She don't look like she wants to do it."

Yes! That's right, Owen! Tell him! And tell him to set me free while you're at it!

"It don't matter if she wants to do it, Owen. That's why she's here."

"Please, Mud! Listen to Owen! Please let me go!" I tried begging again, alternating my pleading eyes between the two men.

"Shut up!" Mud shouted at me. He turned his attention back to Owen. "You're ready for this. Do it just like in the movie and you'll be good."

Heavy tears flowed down my cheeks and under my chin. The neckline of my shirt began to get soaked.

"See, she's already playing along."

I curled up into a tighter ball and hooked my wrists around my legs. He had been training Owen by showing him rape porn. He wanted me to cry. He wanted me to be scared. And I'm sure he wanted me to fight back. I wished I had the strength to not give him what he wanted.

"Maybe later," Owen said even slower than his already hesitant cadence. I saw he didn't want to hurt me. That Mud called the shots. For a moment, I left myself and felt so badly for Owen. To be trapped in a mind that didn't comprehend a lot of things had to be difficult enough already, but then to be manipulated into thinking that something as horrific as this was normal. He knew in his heart it wasn't right, and that was my only silver lining.

"Well, if you're not gonna do it, I am. She's as sweet as a peach and I just gotta pick it! Watch and learn, brother."

I wanted to melt into the wall. He stepped toward the bed and grabbed my ankles, dragging me toward him. I tried to stay upright, but he yanked so hard that I slid to my back. Mud took my arms and shoved them above my head, instructing me to hold onto the bars of the headboard.

"No! No! Oh, God! No! Please don't!" I screamed.

He slapped me across the face. "You want more of that? Do what I said!"

I cried harder and harder, but did as he demanded.

He ran his hands down the length of my arms and then to my breasts, squeezing them aggressively. I cried out in pain, which only seemed to make him more excited. Then in some teasing way, he undid my jeans slowly before peeling them down my legs with a jerk. He licked his lips as he eyed my panties. In an instant, his hands were inside them, his fingers exploring me. Each pass of his rough hands over my delicate flesh was more uncomfortable than the last. I tried pushing him away but stopped when the back of his right hand made contact with my cheek.

"Pay attention, Owen. It's about to get really good." Mud's voice was low and almost seductive. He grabbed the front of my panties and literally ripped them off me. He smiled widely at my embarrassed exposure. "Don't that look tasty?"

I looked at Owen as Mud stood back and unbuckled his belt, catching his eye for a moment before he turned his head. Why was he just standing there?

When my attention turned back to Mud, I was startled to see he had already removed his pants and underwear. Fear coursed through me, thumping my heart at a rapid speed. Tears gushed from my eyes as he forced my legs apart. He was about to take my virginity and there was nothing I could do about it. I squeezed my eyes shut as hard as I could. I just wanted it to be over, and I didn't to see him on top of me.

I cried out as he slammed himself into me the first time. He grunted with each thrust, acting out his perverted fantasy while waves of tears flowed down the side of my face.

"Tell me you like it," he groaned in my ear. When I didn't respond, he got even closer to my ear and upped the ante. "Tell me you like it, or I'm gonna gut you like a fish when I'm done."

For a second, death seemed preferable, but I wanted to make it out of there alive. My mother's voice rang through my mind again: *Be brave. Even when you're scared, be brave.*

"I like it," I finally mumbled through my sobs.

And just like that, he gave one final grunt and collapsed on top of me. After a minute, he stood up, put his underwear and pants back on, and moved toward the door.

"And that, dear brother, is how it's done."

Owen looked me as if he wasn't sure what to make of what he'd witnessed. His eyes were wide and his mouth was agape. Mud ushered him out and left, closing the door behind them.

Taking my place back in the corner, I rested my forehead on my knees and continued to cry. Through my soft sobs I heard the sounds of my entrapment: *squeak, tap, click.*

Day 100

As promised, Officers Day and Moore returned to the hospital this morning with a list of questions, each a rewording of one from the day before.

How long do you think you were out in the back of the truck?

How far away do you think he took you?

How long did you walk through the woods before you got to the main road?

How long did you walk along the road before you were picked up?

What did Mud look like?

Does Mud have any distinguishing marks?

What did the house look like?

Was the house big or small?

I could answer the questions about Mud's appearance with certainty. He was about six feet tall, had brown hair and brown eyes. He looked like every other man I knew: handsome but rough around the edges. My answers to most of the other questions were guesses, which, by the expressions on the officers' faces, were not going to prove helpful.

Nurse MaryKay had already been in to let me know they were releasing me. They called my father and he would be there soon to get me.

"We've also made a call to the hospital closest to Pinewood in Clary. They have an excellent counseling department and run a group for survivors," MaryKay said. She handed me a piece of paper with the hospital name and number on it.

"Thanks." I took the paper and set it on the table hovering above the bed. "Um ... can I please have towel? I'd like to take another shower before my dad gets here."

"You took three showers yesterday, and the nightshift said you were up at 3:00 am taking another one."

"Yeah, I know." I wrung my hands together, not sure why I even asked. "I just ... I can't get clean enough."

MaryKay made a tight line with her lips and looked at me with soft eyes. "Of course. I'll get you some clean scrubs to wear home, too."

I swallowed hard and nodded my appreciation.

Dad walked into my room as I dried my hair with the towel.

"Are we going to run out of hot water at home?" He asked with a soft smile.

"Probably," I told him.

"That's just fine with me," he said. I laid the towel on the bed and met him half way across the room, letting his arms wrap around me. I was safe and secure there, and as long I had them around me, I would eventually be okay.

We stopped by the nurses' station on our way out so I could say thank you. They had all been so kind and gentle with me.

"You take care, Caroline," my main nurse, MaryKay, said. "You're a survivor if I've ever seen one."

She hugged me sweetly and the other nurses patted and rubbed my back, expressing similar sentiments.

I climbed in Dad's truck and inhaled deeply. It smelled like him. It smelled like home. Home. I couldn't wait to get home. I wanted to see the farm and smell the animals. I wanted to take the steps up to the porch and open that old screen door. And I wanted to walk into my house and see my mom in her recliner. Most of all, I couldn't wait to throw my arms around her.

"Everyone is real excited to see you," Dad said.

"They know what happened?" I asked, staring out the window.

Dad hesitated before he answered. "They put it together."

I nodded and wondered how many of them would avert their eyes from me. How many would look past me as they spoke to me? *If* they spoke to me. And what about me? How I would I react to them knowing the horrors I had endured? I had grown up around big, burly men on the farm my whole life. And not for one millisecond had I ever been afraid of any of them. After I had experienced the evil men were capable of, would I be able to look at *them* the same way?

We drove through the middle of Pinewood, past Renfrow's and Anderson's. A banner across the front window of Anderson's read, "Welcome Home, Caroline!" It was sweet, but after registering it, my eyes found the parking space Mud's truck had been in. Fortunately, we passed it pretty quickly and were on the other side of the small town square in no time.

Butterflies filled my stomach as we approached the road to the farm. When I expected Dad to slow down for the turn, he didn't. He passed it and kept going.

"You missed the turn, Dad," I said. He was probably lost in thought.

"We have to make a stop before we go home," he told me.

"But I really want to see Mom," I said.

"Don't worry. You'll see her soon."

I figured he was taking me straight to the hospital in Clary to get me registered for that group or something. Or get me signed up for counseling. I just wanted to go home, but I guess it was best to get it set up and out of the way. Once at home, I had no plans of leaving my mother's side any time soon.

We drove another 30 minutes and turned onto Settler's Pass, a worn out road that took you straight to the pond on the edge of the Rourke's land. You could see the huge chestnut tree beside the pond all the way from the main road. It was beautiful, and my mother's favorite place to read on a summer day as a kid.

After a bumpy few minutes, my father brought the truck to a stop. He unbuckled his seatbelt and got out, not saying a word. It wasn't like Dad to be so mysterious, but we were both different after what happened.

I got out and followed him. Each silent step he took toward the tree fed my curiosity. He finally stopped a few feet from the tree and turned around. He looked at me for a moment then he looked over his shoulder. I followed his eyes and saw nothing, so I walked around him to the other side of the massive trunk.

There, protruding from the ground, was a simple tombstone with my mother's name on it. I dropped to my knees.

"When?" I cried.

My father was quickly beside me, his arm around my shoulders. "Four weeks ago."

"But … Dr. Connor … the experimental medication," I said.

"He said there were no guarantees."

I cried harder. "She still should have had more time, even without it," I offered.

Dad pulled me closer to him. "Her body was under a tremendous amount of stress. It was just not a good recipe."

Stress. Because of me. No. Because of Mud. He killed her.

When they find him, I hope they hang him.

We sat there and cried together for a long time before we sat in the silence of our sadness. Dad cried for me not having been able to say goodbye to Mom. I cried for Dad having to go through Mom's death all by himself. And we both cried as we grieved the loss of one of the world's truly perfect people.

By the time we pulled onto our road, the redness around my eyes had nearly disappeared. I'd most likely cry myself to sleep that night, but for the moment, I was sort of okay.

We rounded the bend and the big elm tree. Our home came into view and my saddened heart began to ease. Cheers and hollering erupted, welcoming me home. The whole farm staff crowded out there, beaming from ear to ear. Some of the brawniest of them wiped tears.

I got out of the car and smiled. No one tried to hug me—probably on the instructions of my father—but they clapped and whistled and said how happy they were I was home.

We entered the house, and my eyes immediately flew to Mom's recliner in the front living room. I had to sit in it. I had to be close to her again. My eyes still fixed on the chair, I headed into the living room.

"Hi, Caroline." Peter stood from the couch.

"Hi, Peter," I said. Seeing him made my arrival home complete. I stepped closer so I could hug him, but he stepped away from me. I looked down, embarrassed. He knew what happened to me and couldn't be near me. "It's okay. I get it."

"No. It's not what you think," he said. His eyes were turned down and red from crying, and he clenched his jaw. A tear rolled down his left cheek. "I am *so* sorry, Caroline."

"Why are you sorry?"

"If I hadn't taken so long with Sonny, I would have been there and that asshole wouldn't have taken you. You're my family, and I'm supposed to protect you. I didn't protect you. I got there and you were gone. Your cell phone was on the ground, and you were nowhere. I shouldn't have taken so long! I'm so, so sorry!" Peter's body dropped into the chair behind him, his face falling into his hands.

"Oh my God, Peter! It's not your fault!" I rushed to his side. "It's no one's fault but his!"

"I've spent the last three months praying you were okay and thinking of ways to make it up to you," he said through his tears.

"You don't have anything to make up for. I don't blame you for anything that happened," I told him. He looked up at me, his eyes a little brighter. "I promise."

Peter threw his arms around me and held me tight. Peter was my cousin, but he was also my best friend. It broke my heart to know he had spent all that time thinking my kidnapping had been his fault.

The list of ways Mud had destroyed my life grew. He had to be found and taken down. The only way that would happen was if I could remember all the details the police asked me about before. I decided my first step of survival would be to write down everything I could remember. If I had to go back to each moment and remember each horrific detail, I would. All that mattered was that Mud paid for what he did to me.

Day 5

Squeak. Tap. Click.

Those quickly became my three favorite sounds. Each one meant Mud had ended Owen's lesson on *how to be a man*, and I could lie there in my despair.

I tried to escape every time he opened the door, so Mud attached a long chain to the bed and then handcuffed me to it. I got as far as a foot over the threshold once. At first he just yanked me back into the room and threw me on the bed. After the fourth or fifth time, he was pretty pissed. He grabbed a fist full of my hair and slammed my head into the doorframe before tossing me on the ground and kicking me in the side a few times. I stopped trying to escape after that.

He also said I had to bathe because I was starting to stink. When I told him it was his fault, he slapped me across the face. That's when I gingerly pointed out the fact that I couldn't shower with the cuff on.

"She ain't goin' nowhere, Mud. You could take it off so she can shower," Owen offered. Thank God for Owen's voice of reason. Mud agreed to uncuff me, but not before he gave me a stern warning.

"If you so much as breathe in the direction of that door, I'll make sure you don't walk for a week." Mud's eyes were dark and evil, and I believed every word he said. "Be quick. I ain't got all morning."

Handcuffs. I wondered if he was a cop. Wouldn't that be perfect?

I turned the shower on as hot as it would go, which still wasn't hot enough. The only thing available to wash my hair and body was a bar of Dove soap. Not that I cared. All I wanted was to wash Mud off and out of me. That was harder to do that I thought it would be. My body was sore from head to foot. Even my lathered hands gliding over my skin caused me to flinch. Bruises had formed on my inner thighs from where he dug his knees in to keep my legs spread. And my scalp and face and neck were tender to the touch after Mud's repeated yanking of my hair and backhanded slaps.

I wasn't as clean as I wanted to be. Being dipped in a vat of sanitizer might never achieve that. But I got out and wrapped the towel around me because I didn't want to face Mud's wrath if I took too long. I didn't have a brush, so I just combed my fingers through my hair and tried to get out as many tangles as possible. Once dry, I put my dirty shirt and jeans back on. It was better than being naked.

I had taken as quick a shower as I could, considering my bruised state. When Mud came back into the bedroom, I was as ready as I could ever be to have him slap the cold metal around my wrist again. Without a word, he cuffed me and left.

Squeak. Tap. Click.

I sat on the bed and put my face in my hands. I still couldn't understand how I got there. How had I been fooled? I was just trying to help. The tears fell as I thought about Mom. She was already under so much stress. My disappearance couldn't be good for her, especially in between treatments. I prayed she would hang on.

A light knock sounded at the door—Owen. Mud was never so polite as to knock. He had left to do whatever it was that kept him from raping me all day.

Click. Squeak.

Owen opened the door slowly, one hand on the doorknob, the other holding a plate with a peanut butter and jelly sandwich and a short glass of milk, like he had twice a day since Mud took me there. But that time, he spoke to me.

"Here you go," he said as he set the plate on the bed and put the glass of milk on the nightstand. He gave me a polite nod and turned to leave.

"You don't watch," I said hesitantly. Just because he hadn't shown any signs of aggression like Mud didn't mean he wasn't capable. I had to tread lightly. He stopped in his tracks. It was an odd choice for my first words outside of "thank you" to him, but it had been an important observation I made from the beginning.

"No ma'am," he said before turning around. "But please don't tell Mud that. He'd be awful mad."

"Why would he be mad?"

"Cuz I'm not bein' a good learner."

"Well, if you let me go, you wouldn't have to worry about that. You could just go back to watching your movies." I pulled the sandwich apart nonchalantly, glancing up at Owen to gauge his response.

"Oh, no ma'am. I don't think Mud would like that very much," he replied. He turned to leave.

"No, you're right," I said in hopes of stopping him. Owen was my only chance to make it out alive. "He takes care of you, doesn't he?"

Owen turned around. "Yes, ma'am."

"Is it just the two of you who live here?" I asked. I needed to start gathering information.

"No, ma'am. This is my house," he answered. He leaned casually against the doorframe. "Mud lives up the trail on the other side of the trees."

"Oh." The wheels in my head started turning. "So it's just us here at night then?" Own nodded. "Why don't you come in to see me at night?"

He looked down sheepishly. "I reckon you need your rest."

"That's very sweet of you." I took a bite of the sandwich I'd been turning over in my hands. He smiled and blushed.

"Is night the only time Mud isn't here?" I needed to gauge my windows of opportunity.

"Mud goes to work most of the time," he said.

"Most of the time?"

"Once in a while his leg acts up and he can't work, but he goes most days."

So he *had* been limping when he carried me in from the car.

"That's too bad. How did he hurt it?" *Accosting another unsuspecting young girl?*

[33]

In a flash, Owen's sweet demeanor changed. He rocketed himself away from the wall and stepped toward me. His arms were straight down at his side and his fists were clenched. I flinched back, startled.

Oh no. What had I done? Was he really that sensitive about how Mud hurt his leg, or had I inadvertently done something else to spark his aggression?

"You need to finish your food," he snapped. He took the plate and then picked up the glass of milk, shoving it my direction. A quarter of it sloshed onto the floor. He examined the mess and furrowed his brow.

"I'm sorry, Owen. I didn't mean to upset you," I said.

His eyes shifted in thought before he spoke. "No. I'm sorry."

"It's okay." I smiled softly at him. Last thing I needed was Owen to turn on me. I took the glass from him and took a few big gulps, followed by a big bite of sandwich. Within a minute I had consumed both.

"Owen?" I called as he began to pass through the door. "Do you think you could take the handcuff off me?"

"Mud says you have to wear it if he's not here," he said.

"Why only then?" I asked.

"Mud says you'll try and trick me into leaving."

"I would never trick you, Owen. You've been nothing but kind to me." Owen blushed and bowed his head. "Thank you for the sandwich and milk. It's very kind of you to take care of me. I want you to know how much I appreciate it."

"You're welcome, Miss…"

"Caroline. My name is Caroline."

99 Days

Neither Owen nor Mud had asked my name once in the five days I had been there. Mud only barked orders and had his way with me. Owen did everything he could to avoid talking to me.

"You're welcome, Miss Caroline." Owen smiled and closed the door behind him.

Squeak. Tap. Click.

I lay down on the bed with my head at the foot and looked out the narrow windows, the chain attached to the bed coiled on my belly. The branches and leaves of the trees waved wildly in the wind. It reminded me of lying under the big elm tree at home.

I, hopefully, had several hours before Mud would be back for round two of my daily torture. With no clock anywhere to be seen, I had a hard time gauging time. During the time I had to myself, I had figure out how to persuade Owen to let me go. His loyalty to Mud ran so deep, and I wasn't convinced he'd ever turn on him.

A knock at the door startled me. I sat up and automatically moved to the corner of the bed by the wall. I was already so well trained.

Click. Squeak.

"You look like you're smart, so I brought you a book," Owen said as he stepped into the room, a paperback book at the end of his extended arm. I took the book from him and read the title: *James and the Giant Peach*.

"Whose book is this?" Oh my God! Were there were kids nearby?

"It's mine," he answered.

"Oh," I answered, relieved. It was kind of sweet that he kept his childhood books. Mom kept every book she read as a child and passed them on to me. "Did you like it?"

[35]

"I haven't read it."

"It's good. I read it in fourth grade. I like all Roald Dahl's books."

Awkward silence.

"I got all his books, if you want to read somethin' different," he offered.

"Why don't you pick your favorite one and I'll read that?" I said.

"I haven't read any of them," Owen replied.

A grown man with a set of children's books he'd never read. If he wasn't keeping them for posterity's sake, why have them at all? Unless there *were* children around, at which thought my fear for their lives skyrocketed. "Why not?"

He looked down and shuffled his feet.

"Owen?"

Still, he averted his eyes. That's when I understood.

"Owen? Do you know how to read?"

Owen shook his head, which still hung down.

Before I could say anything the door to the house creaked open and slammed closed. Mud's heavy, limping footsteps boomed louder as he made his way down the hall to my room. Owen snatched the book from me, shoved it in the back of his pants, and turned toward the door. I scrambled to the corner of the bed and pulled the blanket over my body and up to my chin, an instinctive reaction anytime Mud approached.

"All right! Owen, my man!" he exclaimed. He saw Owen inside the room and assumed that Owen had finally conquered me. "So? How was it?"

Owen looked at me and then back at Mud and then shrugged.

"It's all right, little brother. The more you do it, the better you get. Aren't you glad I brought her here? You're a real man now, Owen." Mud nodded his head sharply and left the room. "C'mon! I wanna hear all about it." he called back.

Owen swallowed hard as he took my shaking figure in. I think we were both afraid of what Mud would do had he seen that we were discussing children's books. I put my forehead on my knees and tried to breathe, tried to calm my nervousness.

Squeak. Tap. Click.

I raised my head, took a deep breath, and sighed when I saw it. Sitting on the corner of the bed was Owen's copy of *James and the Giant Peach*.

Day 104

I marched into the Pinewood police station with a chip on my shoulder. I had been home four days and hadn't heard anything from Officers Moore or Day since the hospital. They had all the information they could possibly need. Why hadn't they found him?

"I'd like to speak with Officer Moore, please," I said to the officer at the front desk.

He looked back into the pool of officers and turned back to me. "She's not at her desk. Have a seat and she'll see you when she's back."

I was so pissed off I almost shouted, "Do you know who I am?" but decided against it. So I sat down and waited for Officer Moore to return. Fortunately, that didn't take long.

"Caroline!" she greeted me cheerily. "Come on back." I followed her to an office with a window that looked out to the pen of men and women in blue. She closed the door behind me and waved to a chair as an offer to sit. I sat calmly and looked up at her with anticipation. "What can I do for you today?"

"What can you do for me? You can find the asshole who held me captive and raped me. That's what you can do." My tone was intentionally sharp. "Why haven't you found him yet?"

Officer Moore sat in the chair next to me and let out a heavy sigh. "I know it's difficult, the waiting. You're not the first victim to express that. But I have to ask you to please be patient. There's a lot of ground to cover, literally. And with the storm that blew through the other day, even your tracks are long gone. I promise we are doing everything we can. And I *promise* we will find him. I need you to trust me."

I put my face in my hands and suppressed the scream begging to be released. It had been five days since I sprinted from the little house and ran aimlessly into the woods. I lay in a hospital bed, delusional enough to think that once I gave them every detail I could remember, they'd go out there and find him.

I felt Officer Moore's hand on my shoulder. "It's going to be okay."

"No. It's not. Not until you find him." I waved my hands on either side of my head wildly. "*This* won't go away until he's rotting in jail."

"I'm not giving up. He's out there and we're going to get him."

You better.

I pulled down the long driveway to our property and decided to go see Peter instead of heading for the house. Peter was extra busy as we closed in on slaughter season, so I hadn't seen him much. Dad, either. I think everyone on the farm tried to give me space, actually. But I missed Peter the most. He had been my best friend, and I couldn't have been happier to get back to him.

The truck came to a halt in a cloud of dust. Peter stood outside the slaughter building giving Maricio instructions on something. As soon as I walked up, Maricio nodded politely at me and walked into the building.

"Hey," I said to Peter.

"Hey," he said curtly back before walking away from me and into the building.

"How's it going?" I walked behind him and tried to catch up.

"It's good. Busy. I'm training Maricio and Johnny on the new cap bolt guns. We got new ones in…" He stopped and turned around quickly. "I'm super busy, Caroline. Is there something you need?"

"Um … no. I just wanted to come see you. I totally get it, though. Wanna hang out and watch a movie or something tonight?" I asked, trying to salvage the conversation.

"I can't. Early morning tomorrow and my mom needs me to help her with some stuff tonight."

"Oh, well, I could come over there and help," I offered. I desperately didn't want to be alone. Dad barely spoke to me. He seemed unsure what to say, and I had no clue where to start with him. Mom had always been our common denominator. I needed Peter.

"Another time. Okay?" I noted the dismissive gesture of checking his watch and turned to leave. "Caroline?" I spun around, my eyes wide with hope. I studied Peter's face while I waited for him to say something. His mouth opened and closed slightly, like he was looking for the words to say. "I'll catch you later."

I nodded. "Sure."

My best friend, my own cousin, couldn't stand to be around me. He didn't even know how to talk to me anymore. When he looked at me, he saw a victim. I thought I would come home and pick up the pieces of my life. And I thought the people I loved would be there to help me pick those pieces up. Instead, I had become a leper.

My heart was broken.

Day 105

I really don't want to be here.

I sat in the sterile waiting room in a chair made more uncomfortable by my injuries, waiting to talk to a shrink, because my father had already been through enough. And because my mother was gone. If she were still alive, hers would be the only ears I needed. She would have the only words I wanted to hear. Maybe that'd be where I started: the fact that Mud didn't just take me away from my home, but he robbed me of saying goodbye to my mother. Of course, I may not have had to say goodbye to her so soon had my disappearance not caused her so much pain.

"Caroline?" The woman calling my name was dressed neatly in a pair of navy pants, a white dress shirt, and a tailored navy jacket. Her hair was pulled back in a low ponytail, and her makeup minimalistic.

"That's me," I said as I stood.

She extended her hand as I approached. "I'm Dr. Skendari, but you can call me Wendy."

"Okay ... Wendy."

"You know, most girls choose to go to group sessions with other survivors," she said.

"I know. I'm not interested in sitting around listening to other girls recount their horror stories. Mine is enough for me," I said.

"Well, maybe you'll change your mind."

I followed Wendy to her office and sat in the chair she motioned to as she closed the door. This chair was soft, much more comfortable than the one I had just been in, and sat opposite its identical twin. I took a deep breath while I waited for Wendy to get something from her desk and meet me in the head-shrinking zone. I had an idea of how it would go. She'd ask me first to tell her what happened and then to talk about how I felt about it. I couldn't imagine I'd come to any shocking realizations in the process. I had my life and my virtue ripped away from me. I felt all the feelings.

Wendy sat, crossed her legs, and flipped open a leather notebook. "Before we start I wanted to give you the card of a colleague of mine. She works with parents who have lost a child or who have a child who has experienced a trauma. It's important that your loved ones get some help in coping with their end of all this." She handed me a card and half sheet of paper with information for a parental support group.

"I'll give it to him, but I'm not sure he'll come," I said. "He's really busy on the farm and, well, he's not super big on talking about his feelings. Don't get me wrong, he's always been an awesome dad, and we've always been close. But, well, he's a rancher."

"When he's ready, hopefully he'll come around. Now, how about we start with an introduction?" she said. "A little about me: I've been a psychiatrist for 20 years, and have been working with victims of sexual assault for the last seven. I've pretty well seen and heard it all."

"You get a lot of girls who have been kidnapped and been used as personal blow-up dolls?" I was snarky and I didn't care.

"No, actually," she said, unfazed by my attitude. "But I'm glad to see you feel comfortable enough to say exactly what's on your mind. That will be important to your progress." We exchanged looks. "Being angry and pissed off at what happened to you is totally understandable. It's also perfectly acceptable."

I crossed my arms. "You think I'm angry about what he did to me?"

"Aren't you?" she posed. "He took you from your home, your mother and father. Took your virginity."

"I don't care about my virginity," I lied.

"What do you care about?"

"I care that I'm home. I just want to move on with my life," I said.

"Moving past trauma is difficult. It involves reliving some terrible things, talking about those who caused you pain, and taking control away from them," she explained.

"I *don't* want to talk about him. And I'm not giving him a single molecule of my emotions." I fought back tears.

"All right. So you're not angry with him for raping you and stealing your virginity. What are you angry about?" Wendy asked.

"Not being there when my mother died," I answered.

"Let's start there, then," Wendy offered.

"With what? My mom dying?"

"That seems to be the most pressing thing for you right now so, yes. Let's talk about your mom dying."

Wendy tilted her head as she waited for me to say something. Was this the part where I spilled my guts? I was relieved, though, that she wasn't making me talk about Mud. I wanted to leave all that behind. However delusional it may have sounded to someone else, I felt like I could get past being repeatedly raped. I wasn't sure if I'd ever get over not being there when Mom died.

"I don't know what to say," I finally told her.

"I understand your mother had been sick," Wendy said.

"She had cancer. The chemo hadn't worked, but she was supposed to start some experimental treatment," I said. "We worked everything out the day ... the last time I saw her. She only had to wait a few weeks for the chemo to be out of her system, then she could start the new treatment."

"And did she start the new treatment?"

"No." The word left my lips and I felt like I was tattling on my mother.

"Do you know why?" Wendy asked. She jotted something down as she spoke and then concentrated on me.

"It would have required her to be constantly monitored in the hospital. Dad said Mom refused to the leave the house until I came home." My heart quickened. The gut-wrenching vision of my mother sitting in her recliner, wasting away, haunted me. It filled my nightmares.

"How does that make you feel?" Wendy asked.

"I already told you. It makes me angry that I wasn't there when she passed." Was she going to ask me a lot of questions I had already answered?

"I'm wondering how it makes you feel that your mother made the choice to refuse treatment." Wendy's question caught me off guard.

I sat forward in my seat. "She just wanted to be there when I got home!"

"That's the *reason* she made her choice. I'm asking how you *feel* about that choice." Wendy softened her voice and her eyes.

I knitted my brows together, and then felt all the muscles in my face drop.

"I hate it," I said quietly. "I wish she had listened to Dad. He tried to convince her to go ahead with treatment, but she was more afraid of not being there when I got home than of dying."

"Do you think she would have gone forward with the treatment if you had been there?" Wendy posed.

"Yes." I answered without hesitation. Mom may have been preparing for the worst, but she was willing to try. I sat back in my seat and crossed my legs.

"So, while you were in a house in the middle of nowhere being raped, your mother lay in bed dying. Dying because she made a choice to refuse treatment so she would be right where you left her when you got home. Her choice, but who created the scenario where she had to make that decision?"

Tears streamed down my face. Dammit. I didn't want to talk about him and what he did to me. I had even stopped uttering his name when I talked to the police. I wanted to leave him behind, but in ten minutes,

Dr. Wendy had made it clear that wasn't possible. Not if I ever hoped to move on with my life.

"Mud." I said his name through clenched teeth.

"And how do you feel about Mud?"

"I hate him."

Day 11

Mud gave a final thrust, pulled out of me, and groaned as he came on my back. The last few days, this had been his preferred position. It became mine as well because it meant I didn't have to look at his disgusting face or have his gross, sweaty body on top of me. But taking me from behind didn't mean he couldn't still utter his choice of sweet nothings in my ear. That day's poetic genius was, "Your cunt is so tight."

I had stopped crying, at least while he raped me. I started thinking part of what got him off was seeing me distraught. I started saving it for the shower. The anxiety of not knowing when he would enter my dungeon had caused a lot of my tears. It took a few days to realize that his sporadic arrival was due to the weekend. Once the workweek arrived Mud opened the bedroom door like clockwork. He came in every morning before work and every evening after. That gave me a solid eight hours to continue working on Owen. Of everything I'd considered as a plan of escaping, Owen continued to be my only hope.

Mud let me shower every three days and that day was a showering day. I extended my arm behind me and he uncuffed me. I stayed bent over the bed so the disgusting fluid resting on my back wouldn't slide down me while Mud buckled his pants.

Squeak. Tap. Click.

As soon as I heard the click of the lock, I rushed into the small bathroom, turned the shower to the hottest setting, and jumped in. The water was cold at first, but I didn't care. The point was to get *him* off me. On days when he didn't let me take a full shower, I filled the sink up and washed as much of him away as I could. The temperature in the shower warmed up and I stretched my neck under the water while trying to sterilize my skin with the heat. Those were the times I allowed myself to cry. It felt like they were always big, gushing tears, but under the shower, I'd never know.

I dried myself off and combed my hair through with the comb Owen had brought me two days earlier. Even though I had been able to wash my hair, running my fingers through it hadn't been sufficient to keep it from turning into a nest. I put on the white t-shirt Owen had also given me and scratched another hash mark on the back of the bathroom door with the edge of my handcuff before I returned to the bed.

Mud returned a few moments later, cuffed me, and left.

I didn't start keeping track of the days until day five. I had lost count of how long I had been there, but added it up by recalling what Mud had said to me each day. Day one he told me to say I liked it or he'd gut me like a fish. Day two he told me to tell him I liked it again. Day three Mud instructed me to take his pants off and tell him how big his penis was. When I refused, he backhanded me across the face. Day four he told me to chant things like "deeper" and "harder." I hesitated, so he grabbed a fist full of my hair and pulled my head back with what felt like all his might.

All of this happened while Owen stood at the door and pretended to watch.

Owen.

I oscillated between feeling sorry for him and hating him as much as I did Mud. He was there with me all day and could let me go at any time, but didn't. He was just as afraid of Mud as I was. Afraid of what would happen if we didn't do as Mud said. Every day I wondered what it would take for Owen to see Mud for who he really was: a violent, sadistic rapist. Until that day came, I would be trapped here.

Tap. Squeak.

Owen tapped on the door before he opened it. He always wanted to be sure I was as dressed as I could be. He set a plate of toast with cheese and a glass of milk on the nightstand and then left the room. He returned quickly with a stack of laundry.

"I washed some towels," he said as he set the stack at the foot of the bed. "And I found some of these for you." He held out his hand with some small, cottony items while turning his head toward the door. I took what he offered and half smiled.

"These are underwear, Owen. Women's underwear. Where did you get them?" I asked.

"Um ... I know a girl and got them from her," he answered shyly.

My eyes widened. "Did you tell her who they were for?"

Owen looked down. "She don't know I took them."

"Owen."

"I'm sorry. I never stole nothin' in my life!" he explained. "It's just … you only had the one pair and my momma always said clean underpants was the most important thing. 'You can't be clean without clean underpants,' she'd always say."

I sighed at the sweetness of his gesture. In the midst of everything, he was concerned for my hygiene.

"Thank you, Owen. This is very kind of you." I smiled softly.

Owen's demeanor brightened at my recognition of his good deed. "I washed your jeans and your shirt, too!"

"Thank you," I said. I turned my attention to the breakfast Owen had brought me. Taking the plate from the nightstand, I lifted the cheese toast to my lips. After a few bites, I took a long sip of milk. "Do you have a new book?" I asked. We finished *James and the Giant Peach* on Friday. Mud was in and out of the house over the weekend, so Owen and I agreed to wait to start a new story until Monday.

"This one?" Own pulled a small paperback from his back pocket and held it out for me to see.

"Another Roald Dahl? All of his books are wonderful," I said taking the book from him. "*The Twits*. Not as well-known as his other books, but a great one just the same. I remember liking this one a lot when I was a kid."

I set the book down and finished my breakfast. I considered the book sitting next to me and remembered how my mother used to read to me. Story time was special. Mom helped me become a lover of books and began teaching me how to read with story time. She always picked books with lessons that were applicable to real life. I couldn't remember any life lesson I could extrapolate from *The Twits* to help

Owen see he should let me go, but I hoped there would be something in another book that would open the door. Owen was so loyal to Mud, but he was also naïve. I hated to take advantage of his disability, but I'd do whatever I had to in order to get home.

"Thank you for the cheese toast. I haven't had that in a long time. It was very good," I said to Owen as I handed him my dishes.

"You're welcome, Caroline," Owen said. He took the dishes from me and left the room. He left the door open, which he had never done before, so I went as far as the chain would let me, stood quietly, and looked out into the rest of the house. My room was at the end of a short hall. I could see another door up and to the left, and then the back of a recliner at the edge of what must have been the living room. A hallway down and to the right from my room, I surmised, led to the door Mud brought me through.

The dishes clanked in the kitchen sink at the end of the hall, startling me back to the moment. I wasn't afraid of what Owen would do if he saw me in the doorway, but I couldn't afford for him to become suspicious and lose our rapport.

I scurried into the bathroom and pushed the door so it hid the toilet from view. Owen's footsteps got louder. I counted to ten and then flushed. When I came out, Owen stood near the door. His head was down, but I could see his face flushed a little red with embarrassment.

"Are you ready?" I asked. Owen nodded and we sat on the side of the bed near the foot. "*The Twits*." I opened the cover of the book and read. "Mrs. Twits."

After I had read the two short paragraphs on that page, I turned to the first chapter.

"It's true," Owen said before I began reading again.

I looked at him, confused. "What's true?"

"It's true that if a person has ugly thoughts, they turn ugly."

"Who do you know that thinks ugly thoughts?" I held my breath and waited for him to say his brother's name. No one on earth had uglier thoughts than Mud.

"My momma and daddy had ugly thoughts," he explained. "They had ugly thoughts about me." His face looked dejected as he dropped his chin.

"Oh. Well, sometimes even parents say things they don't mean, Owen."

"They meant them. But they're gone now, so it's okay." Own took the book from me and flipped through the pages.

"I'm so sorry," I said. I patted his shoulder. "I'm sure they're in heaven watching over you."

"Don't be sorry. And they ain't in heaven. They're in hell. Right where Mud put them."

My heart stopped for a second. "What do you mean Mud put them in hell?" I shifted my body and turned toward Owen. He continued to avoid looking right at me; instead, he turned more pages in the book.

"Daddy was beatin' me with a belt again, callin' me a retard, like he did almost every day. Mud grabbed Daddy's shotgun and killed him right then and there. When Momma tried to stop him, Mud shot her, too." Owen finally lifted his head. His eyes caught mine, which happened next to never, and he waited for my reply.

"How old were you?" I asked.

"Thirteen."

"And how old was Mud?"

"Twenty-eight," he answered. "Mud says he saved my life."

"He saved your life." The echoed statement left my lips in a conflict of joy and defeat.

"Yes, ma'am."

It all made sense now. Owen owed his life to his brother. How would I ever convince him to go against Mud?

I took the book from Owen and turned to the first chapter. I held back tears as I began to read aloud. I was never going home.

Day 200

I dried myself off after my morning shower and pulled my hair down from the messy bun I had thrown it in. I threw on a pair of jeans and a t-shirt, and then slipped on my shoes before going downstairs. I landed at the bottom of the stairs and sighed. It had been a rough night. Worse than usual. Not that things had been smooth sailing since I'd come home, but for some reason, everything hit me at once the night before.

I had trouble falling asleep and thought I should have taken Dr. Wendy up on her offer to write me a prescription for a sleep aid. As I often did when I couldn't sleep, I thought of my mother. I thought of how hard she had been fighting to beat her cancer. And I thought of how she might even be better now had she not refused the experimental treatment. And then I thought about how empty the house felt without her.

But I'd turned my thoughts to my father. Before I left, we had always been a close family. He left Mom and me to all the "girl stuff" but made sure I never felt excluded in the field or the barn. I had always helped out in some way on the farm, but when I turned 14, he raised the bar. He taught me how to shoot a gun and a rifle. And he brought me into the slaughter building during slaughter season. Until then, I knew what happened in there, but I'd never seen it.

He explained that it was our responsibility to be as humane as possible. And that, because they were treated so humanely from birth to death, those cows would provide quality nourishment to people all over the country. His beautiful words didn't make it any easier when I pulled the trigger of a cap bolt gun for the first time, shooting a sharp cylinder of steel into the cow's brain. Still, I understood its purpose, and it got easier each time.

Those memories made me so happy. And then they made me angry. What happened to me erased all that and left only a dirty version of me. I had hidden myself away from my father and everyone else, making things even more awkward when I did see Dad or Peter. I didn't want it to be like that anymore. I wanted to move on with my life and get back what I once had. So, instead of sheltering myself in the house all day, or leaving the property all together, I decided to re-enter the life I used to have. I was going to get back out on the land and help out, like I always had.

I found Dad out in the field like he always was at that time of morning. He went out every day to check the grass to make sure it was healthy and to see if any areas needed to be blocked off and seeded. Dad said sometimes the cows find a sweet spot of grass and pull up even the smallest blades. He also checked the perimeter of the land for any breaches in the fence or weak spots. I checked the time and knew he'd be back from the perimeter.

"Hey Dad," I said as I approached him from behind. When he turned around, his eyes lit up with surprise.

"Caroline!" he said. "What are you doing here? Is everything okay?"

"Yeah, I'm fine." Well, mostly. "I thought I'd come and give you a hand." I smiled sheepishly, knowing my out-of-the-blue presence had taken him off guard.

Dad opened his mouth to speak, but it took him a moment to form any words.

"Oh, well, that's very nice of you, but I'm all covered. I hired some new folks a couple months back, so..." He didn't know what to say next after rejecting my offer.

"That's, okay," I said. I tried hard not to show my disappointment. "I'll just hang out with you, then." *Like when I was little. Remember that, Dad? Remember when I was little and not tainted?*

"That'd be great ... except I've got so much to do today that..." He couldn't even finish his sentence. Couldn't even come up with a better excuse. He had no idea the effort it took for me to go out there. If he did, he would have embraced me and made sure I didn't leave his side.

"Sure. I understand." I nodded and turned away before the tears began welling up in my eyes. I didn't want him to see me cry. I didn't want him to change his mind because he felt sorry for me. I wanted him to want me there.

"I'll see you at dinner!" he called out to my back. I raised and hand and waved to him.

I got in the truck and drove to the barn. I wanted to see if we had any new calves. The sweet babies always brought a smile to my face.

When I got there, Peter was walking out. I thought he might offer some relief from my pain, but no. We made eye contact that lasted three seconds before Peter couldn't take it anymore and walked back into the barn. He didn't wave or even mouth a "hello" to me. He turned his back and walked away.

I understood things would be difficult when I got home, but I never imagined the only two people I had left in my life who mattered would treat me that way. Was that how our lives were going to be? Dad pushing me away and Peter pretending I didn't exist? That hurt more than anything Mud ever did to me.

Day 250

"Are you sure there isn't anything else you can remember?" Officer Moore asked for the umpteenth time. I stopped showing up at the police station begging for updates. I started calling every day instead, but that eventually turned into every other day, which turned into once a week, until it was more sporadic than anything. The fiery vengeance I once had all but disappeared. I had the same conversation with Office Moore every time. I'd ask if they were any closer to finding Mud, she'd say no, and then ask if I could remember anything else. Of course, I couldn't.

"No, I'm sorry," I told her.

"We'll get him, Caroline. One day, we'll get him."

One day. One day was way the hell out there and didn't bring me any comfort.

I'd been seeing Dr. Wendy for five months. Some sessions were easier than others. She had this knack for letting me think I decided what we talked about, when in reality she totally drove that train. Even when I was determined not to, she could get me to talk about all the shitty things I felt.

"How's your sleep?" Wendy asked as I crisscrossed my legs in my usual chair.

"Okay, I guess. Still can't shake the nightmares," I said.

"It's only been a few months, Caroline. Give it time," she said.

"And I'm still waking up earlier than I ever did before."

Last week we talked about how conditioned I had become in those 99 days. I didn't need an alarm clock because my body woke up at 6:15 every morning—the time of Mud's first visit. I took a shower almost immediately after waking. But it wasn't until I explained the timing of Mud's afternoon visit that Dr. Wendy was able to explain my compulsion to take another shower at 7:00 pm.

"Are you sure you don't want me to prescribe something?" she asked. Wendy opened the drawer in the small table next to her chair and pulled out a prescription pad. She'd made this offer before but I kept refusing her.

"No, that's okay. I really don't want to be drugged up. My mom took sleeping pills for a little while and it did some crazy things to her." My brain was already fogged up. I didn't need some Ambien-induced hallucinations to go with it.

Wendy put the pad back in the drawer. "If you change your mind, let me know. But also know that I'll most likely ask you again. So, what else would you like to talk about today?"

"You ask that as if I have a choice." I laughed. "It never matters what I do or don't want to talk about. You always have a way of steering the conversation."

"Okay, okay. Fair enough." She laughed. "You haven't brought it up, so I wanted to ask how things were going at home."

"Fine. I mean, everything is pretty status quo. Dad takes care of the farm stuff like always has, and I take care of the me stuff." I give her a tight-lipped smile.

"Do you two talk?"

"About what happened? No," I told her. My father had been through enough. Besides, that's what Dr. Wendy was for.

"Do you two talk about anything?"

"Sure," I answered.

"Like what?"

"Like..." I searched my memory. "I mean..." I shrugged.

We didn't talk. I had been home for months and we barely exchanged ten words a day. He was already up and working when I woke, like he always had been. When he came in for lunch and dinner, I asked how his day was. His reply was always the same: "I woke up with determination, and I'm going to bed with satisfaction." That was Dad's way of saying he accomplished everything he set out to do. After that, the next words we shared were our goodnights. Then we went to bed and got up and did it all again.

"Besides me, who do you talk to? Girlfriends maybe? Your aunts? You've mentioned your cousin Peter," Wendy inquired.

"I was never the type of girl who had a lot of girl friends. And—" I twisted my face. "—my aunts are nice and we're a pretty close family. We're just not *that* kind of close. I always had my mom, so... And Peter? He was my best friend. But things are different now."

"How do you feel they're different?"

Flashbacks of short conversations and Peter's dodgy eyes, along with every hasty exit he'd made since I'd been home scrolled through my mind.

"My mom used to say Peter and I were two peas in a pod. He's only two years older than me and has always been more like a brother than a cousin. We did everything together, and there was a time I could tell him anything. Now? He can't stand to be in the same room, let alone look at me. I walk in, he walks out. When we have tried to talk, he's looking so far up at the ceiling his eyes are about to roll to back of his head. Not that I know what to say to him." I sighed. "I know he feels bad, like it was his fault, even though I told him it wasn't and that I don't blame him."

"Sometimes it can be hard to forgive yourself, even when you've been forgiven. Do you want to be able to talk to him about what happened to you?" Wendy asked then jotted something down quickly.

I thought for a minute before I answered. Did I want to talk to Peter about what happened to me? A pretty loaded question, for sure.

"I don't know. To say yes would mean I wanted to burden him with the knowledge of things I wouldn't wish I my worst enemy. It would mean I was ready for him to see me even more differently than he already does. And knowing just the surface of what happened to me has already made it near impossible for him to look at me. No. I don't want to talk to Peter about what happened to me. I just want to be able to talk to him about the things we used to. Stuff about the farm, his agricultural classes at college, the girls he's interested in. It's been so long now that I don't think we'll ever recover."

Wendy made a note and then brought her attention back to me.

"I have to be honest with you, Caroline. I'm concerned about how isolated you seem to be. You and your father pass like ships in the night, and you and the only other person you've said you could talk to are keeping each other at a distance. You share pretty openly in here with me, but are hesitant with your emotions." Wendy paused. "Do you know how many times you've cried in here? Once, at our first session."

"So the number of times I cry in therapy is some sort of indicator of my recovery?" I snapped.

"We have spoken very specifically about your abuse and you've barely batted an eye. You have so far removed yourself from what happened, you talk about it like it wasn't you. That's your coping mechanism. And while disconnecting and bottling up the feelings may be working for you right now, that bottle can only hold so much. Eventually you're going to explode like someone dropped a Mentos into a bottle of Coke."

"I just want to move on with my life," I said through my clenched jaw.

"What you're doing isn't moving on." Wendy flipped to the back of her notebook and pulled out a half sheet of pink paper she had tucked away there. She held the paper out and I took it from her. "I think it's time for you to connect with other survivors. I'm good at what I do, but you'll never be able to look me in the eye and know I fully understand what you've been through."

I read the bold heading across the top of the paper: SURVIVORS OF SEXUAL ASSAULT SUPPORT GROUP. The group met on the first and third Wednesday of the month in one of the classrooms on the first floor of the hospital from 7:00 pm – 9:00 pm. Tomorrow would be the third Wednesday of the month.

"I don't—"

"Just consider it? At the very least, I'd like you, between now and our next appointment, to think about what's keeping you disconnected from the emotional aspects of your trauma. Can you do that?" Wendy looked at me, hope gazing from her eyes to mine.

I took a deep breath, glanced at the flyer in my hand, and then held it up next to my shoulder. "I'm not making any promises. But yeah, I can think about that."

I shoved the flyer in my purse and we set my next appointment. When I got off the elevator on the first floor, as if it were some kind of sign, I passed right by the classroom that the support group would meet in the very next night.

Driving home I thought about what Wendy had said about me being so disconnected from my feelings. It's true, I didn't ever cry in therapy and worked really hard to keep my emotions in check. But I didn't have to think about why. Owen. If I let go and fell into the emotional abyss of my time in that little room, I would slip up and talk about Owen. I had to safeguard against that. I had to leave him out of it. If I let my guard down, he could be implicated as well and, regardless of what happened, he was the only remotely good thing I had for 99 days. He was the only reason I survived. And I just left him there.

I shook my head and pulled my shoulders to my eyes and dried the tears forming. I would never tell anyone about Owen. Even when they found Mud, I'd deny ever knowing Owen. I wouldn't let him get in trouble for being as much a prisoner as I had been.

I pulled up to the house just after lunchtime. Dad's truck was there, too, but I expected us to pass each other as he headed back out to the field, or wherever he was working on the property that day. I walked into the house and straight to the kitchen to make myself something to eat. Dad was there, and to my surprise, sitting at the kitchen table. In front of him a plate with a sandwich, chips, and a banana, and a tall glass of milk. To his right, in my usual place, was the same. He had cut my sandwich diagonally and separated the way Mom always did it. I appreciated the sweet gesture until I realized what kind of sandwich it was. That's when everything inside me broke.

"Hi Caroline," Dad said. He had a soft smile on his face, and it was the first time since the hospital that he'd looked at me for longer than a few seconds.

"Hi Dad." My heart sank knowing I'd have to reject his kindness. "Thanks for this, but I'm not really hungry." I started to walk away. Dad stood quickly.

"I know it's not the same, but I made your favorite the way your mother used to make it. Please, Caroline. Sit down with me?"

I shook my head, afraid if I spoke, the only thing that would come out were sobs.

"It's just a peanut butter and jelly sandwich with your pop. We don't have to talk or anything. I just ... I know I've been distant, and I'm so sorry. I miss you. I know I haven't been a good father since you got home. I guess I counted on your mother to handle more than I realized."

[65]

"It's not—"

"It's not what? What is it?" he begged. "You want me to make you something else?"

"It's not about your stupid peanut butter and jelly sandwich! I don't ... I can't ..." I ran upstairs, throwing my purse on the floor and myself on my bed.

It was absolutely about that stupid, fucking, peanut butter and jelly sandwich.

Tears soaked my pillow as I cried for the first time outside the safety of a steaming hot shower. Dad knocked on my door and apologized for upsetting me, which made me cry even harder.

"Caroline?" he said softly. "I really am sorry. I didn't mean to upset you." I heard him let out a heavy sigh. "If this is about that support group you gave me the pamphlets for I ... I can try to find time. It's just hard with..." He stopped mid-sentence. "Anyway, I'm sorry."

He had tried to reach out to me, and I ruined everything. Was this what my life would be like? Closed off from the people I love the most and screaming at my father over peanut butter and jelly?

I sat up and dried my face with the hem of my shirt. When I opened my eyes, I saw that the contents of my purse had spilled onto the floor when I dropped it. As I knelt down to clean it up, I couldn't ignore the pink flyer unfolded and lying open, daring me to pick it up. I read the details of the group meeting again.

"Dammit. I guess I'm going to group therapy."

Day 30

The peanut butter seemed extra thick and stuck to the roof of my mouth in a way it hadn't before. It tasted different, too.

"Is this a different brand of peanut butter?" I asked Owen.

"Yes. I'm sorry. Mud said they were out of the kind we normally get, so he got the store brand," he said. "I put extra strawberry jelly on it hopin' you wouldn't notice."

"It's not bad," I said. "The extra jelly helps. Thanks." I washed down the last bite of sandwich with several gulps of milk and handed the dishes to Owen. He returned a minute later with a new book in hand. So far we had read *James and the Giant Peach*, *The Twits*, *Matilda*, and *George's Marvelous Medicine*. With each book I wondered if Roald Dahl had a similar childhood to Owen's. The parents and caretakers in these stories were all awful. But Owen loved them. And the further we read, the more confident Owen became in sounding out words himself. By the time we finished *George's Marvelous Medicine*, he was reading almost a whole page before turning it back to me. It took him almost five minutes to read said page, but he did it himself, and that was pretty cool to watch.

"Is your cheek still sore?" Owen asked.

I reached up and felt my left cheekbone, pushing on it lightly to determine how bruised it still was. A few days ago I had refused Mud's orders to repeat what had become his favorite phrase: "Give it to me harder." I just couldn't say it one more time, but I paid the price for it with the back of Mud's hand flying into my face.

"It's better, thanks," I told him.

"He only does it because he saw our daddy hit our momma."

Yeah. That's why he does it.

We hadn't talked about Owen's parents since they day he told me Mud killed them defending him. My angle of getting Owen to see Mud for the monster he was got shot out of the water the moment he told me that story. I was desperate to find another angle, and I was trying to be brave even though I was scared.

"Owen," I said as sat at the end of the bed. "I want to go home."

Owen put his head down. "I wish I could but…"

"But what? Didn't Mud say I was a gift for you? He's the only one who's … used me." The words fell out of me awkwardly.

"Do you want me to … use you?" Owen asked curiously.

"No," I said quickly. "And I don't think that's what you want either."

"No ma'am." Owen shook his head.

"So, don't you think you can do what you want with your gift?"

"I don't know…"

"My mom is really sick, Owen. And I need to get back to her. How would it be if Mud were sick and someone kept you from getting to him?"

I studied Owen, hoping my reasoning was sinking in. Surely his loyalty to Mud would allow him to understand my desperation. He sat there, silent, with his head down, twisting his fingers together in his lap. I wondered what was going on in that head of his, whether he could even connect the dots like I hoped he would.

After a moment, Owen stood and left the room, closing the door behind him.

My heart sank.

I waited but didn't hear the usual *squeak, tap, click*. I looked around the room, on the floor near the foot of the bed, and even right on the bed where Owen had been sitting to see if he had inconspicuously left the key to my handcuffs, but I didn't see it anywhere. I supposed locking the room was really a moot point anyway. It wasn't like I could leave if I wanted to.

I curled into the corner of the bed and lifted my knees to my chest, defeated. There was no way out unless Owen released me. The window was too small, and there was nothing in the room I could use to jimmy the lock on the handcuffs.

The door opened suddenly, startling me. Owen stood there with my shoes in one hand and my clothes he had washed in the other. He set them on the bed and pulled the key from his pocket. My heart raced with excitement.

"Your momma needs you," Owen said sweetly.

"Oh, Owen! Thank you! Thank you so much!!" I jumped up and held my arm out, the hem of the white undershirt Owen had given me to wear falling just below the waist of my panties. He released the handcuff and I watched as it dropped to the floor with a clank. I rubbed my wrist quickly before grabbing my jeans off the bed. I didn't even care that Owen was still standing there. I thrust each leg into them and fastened them. It wasn't until I needed to take my top off that I stopped and looked at him.

"Right. Sorry," he said shyly before turning toward the door. As soon as his back was turned, I whipped off the old t-shirt Owen had given me to wear and had my bra and shirt on within seconds. My shoes were laced on my feet in as much time and I bolted toward Owen at the door before I knew it.

"Thank you, Owen. You're doing the right thing," I said softly. I touched his shoulder and gave him a wide, thin-lipped smile.

I could hardly believe it. I was free. I needed some idea from Owen as to which direction and how far I would need to go before I found a main road where I could flag someone down.

"I need you to tell me which way to go," I said.

"Out the back, away from the path. It might take you a bit, but you'll come to a highway," he answered.

"Thank you, Owen," I said again.

I stepped out of the bedroom and walked down the hall a few feet. To my right was the small entry Mud had first brought me through. Before I turned, I couldn't help but look ahead into the living room. It was a simple layout with a brown couch and tan recliner, a small rectangular coffee table, and a television. It all looked perfectly normal and nothing at all like the kind of place a sadistic maniac would hold a woman hostage.

To my left was another bedroom. Through the open door, I saw a single bed, neatly made with a wooden nightstand next to it, and a tall, matching dresser. It had to be Owen's room. I looked back at him with sorrowful eyes. After I escaped, this would continue to be his life.

I shook my head to clear it. I had to get focused if I was going to have any endurance to make it through the woods and to safety. That day wasn't a shower day, and I had big plans of delivering Mud's DNA to the police. But before I could take another step, Owen grabbed my arm.

"Wait," he said quickly.

"No, Owen. You can't go back on this now," I said sharply.

"Shhh," he instructed. That's when I heard what Owen had already registered: tires on gravel. The path Owen said to avoid must have been a gravel road. "He's here."

My anxiety-filled heart beat wildly inside my chest. So close and my chance at freedom was being ripped away.

"No, Owen, please. Can't you distract him, or something?" I begged. Tears rolled down my face as Owen pulled me back to the bedroom.

"I can't. I'm sorry," he said. I tried to fight but knew Owen was right. He would have hell to pay for having let me go, but it would be nothing compared to what Mud would do to me.

We scurried back into the room in time to hear the side door fly open. Mud bounded down the short hall and into my room.

"What the fuck is this? Why is she dressed and why *isn't* she cuffed?" he demanded. Mud grabbed my arm and dragged me to the bed. He tossed me down like a rag doll and then secured the handcuff around my wrist again. The clicking of the metal broke my heart.

"He wanted me to get dressed," I said quickly. Mud looked at Owen, waiting for an explanation. I looked at him, too, willing him to play along. The last thing we needed was for Mud to have any clue of what was going on, especially if I wanted a chance of Owen letting me go again.

"Why?" Mud asked incredulously.

Owen searched for how to respond. His loss for words was going to get us caught if I didn't fill in the imaginary blanks.

"He likes it when I strip for him." I stuttered my words so I would sound upset.

Owen looked at me with wide eyes while Mud alternated his gaze between us. There were a good fifteen seconds of silence when I was sure he caught us.

"You know…" Owen finally said. "Like that one movie you said was your favorite."

"I know the one." A disgusting smile crept across Mud's face. "And here I was worried you weren't taking full advantage of my gift."

"Well … I guess I am," Owen said hesitantly.

Mud gave Owen a hearty pat on the back before he leaned against the wall and crossed his ankles. Owen nodded at me once and turned to leave.

"Where're you goin', little brother? Show's about to start!"

"What?" Owen said, surprise written on his face.

"I know I barged in on your party, but don't let me stop you."

Panic coursed through my body.

Why did I have to say that? I should have known Mud would want to see for himself. Poor Owen. Poor Owen? *What is wrong with me? I should be focused on me, not the naïve brother of my captor.* But it was hard not to feel bad for him. He was trapped there with Mud, the brother who thought it was a good idea to train him for sex by showing him porn, followed by kidnapping a girl for him to have unlimited access to all the sex he could dream of. That wasn't what Owen wanted. I knew that better than anyone. But Owen couldn't bring himself to tell Mud himself.

I thought for half a second of spilling all of Owen's beans to Mud, but was too afraid he would think I lied, and I'd get more than the usual hit to my face. I was also concerned for what Mud would do to Owen. It wouldn't have to be physical. A strong reprimand from Mud might possibly be more damaging. But worse was the likelihood of losing the only ally I had. If I betrayed Owen, he would never help me.

"Well, get on with it." Mud opened his arms, palms up, in expectation. I looked at Owen again. His face was frozen in fear.

"Maybe another night, Mud," Owen said. "I'm not really in the mood now."

I let out the breath I had been holding.

"Oh, I see. I spoiled things for you, huh?" Mud said, giving Owen a brotherly punch in the arm.

"Somethin' like that," Owen replied.

"It's all good. I'll have my bit and then she can show me what she does for you tomorrow. Maybe you'll be back in the mood after lunch."

"You mean after dinner," Owen corrected.

"Nope. I'll be around all day for a while. Foreman shut down production at the factory. Somethin' about the health inspector." Mud walked toward me, unbuckling his belt. The look of shock on my face wasn't faked. The safe haven of Mud's work hours had burned to the ground.

Things just got exponentially worse.

Day 251

I'm early. Great.

Normally early is great, but not for this. I stood outside the classroom for the group therapy for survivors, alone, sticking out like a sore thumb to everyone who walked by. Although nothing indicated what was scheduled for the room, I felt like anyone who worked at the hospital knew. I added each person who passed me to the list of those who treated me like a leper.

Maybe I should just leave, I thought. *Maybe they canceled tonight? It's a sign that there's no one here.*

I turned around and was greeted by an overly happy woman in her 40s carrying a large tote and a grocery bag in one hand, and her keys dangling from the other.

"Hey! You must be Caroline!" she said before I could walk past her like I was already walking down the hall.

"Um, yeah," I said, wondering how on earth she knew who I was.

She unlocked the door and answered my mental question.

"Wendy told me she referred you and to keep an eye out," she said.

"Oh. Okay."

I followed her into the classroom. The lights flickered on and illuminated the small space. There was six-foot table on one end of the room and a whiteboard on the other. In the middle sat a circle of chairs. Ten chairs, to be exact.

"I'm Marcia." She extended her hand and I reciprocated, shaking hers. "I'm so glad you chose to come. All the women who have come and gone, and those who still come, find the group to be an integral part of their survival."

"Well, I'm not a big talker, so don't take offense if I'm quiet," I told her.

"No worries. Sometimes it takes a bit for people to warm up to others enough to share. And this is very personal. It's not enough for me to tell you this is a safe place. You have to feel that." Marcia smiled sincerely, which actually made me begin to believe her. *Well played, Marcia. Well played.*

Marcia set up some cookies on the table and pulled bottles of water from a box beneath it. It was low key, but a nice gesture to have a little something.

Five more women arrived after me. They all greeted Marcia by name, so it seemed I was the only new girl. That safe feeling I had diminished.

"Welcome, everyone," Marcia said. "I hope you've all have a good couple of weeks. As you can see, we have a new addition to our group. Everyone, this is Caroline."

I bent my wrist, only slightly lifting my hand off my lap in a pathetic greeting.

"Hi," I said with a mediocre smile. The women looked at me and smiled their greetings. I had never done anything like this, so I had no idea what happened next. Fortunately, Marcia did her job very well.

"So, who would like to start this week? Katie?" Marcia posed.

"Okay, cool, I'll start," Katie said. She was a chubby girl with dirty blonde hair and a bright smile. "Court went really well. It was pretty cut and dried. They showed the security footage from the restaurant's alley and that was it. No jury. The judge asked me if I wanted to make a statement right before he sentenced him to fifteen years. I kept it short and sweet. Told him how he had destroyed my life and that I hoped he rotted in jail for the rest of his life."

Whoa.

"That's pretty harsh, don't you think?" a woman with long, jet-black hair asked.

"Well, Katrina, what I wanted to tell him was that I hoped some big dude in prison made him his bitch, but I refrained. So, no, I don't think what I said was too harsh." Katie rolled her eyes at Katrina.

"I'm glad it went the way you wanted it to go," Marcia said to Katie. "Donna? How about you?"

"Sure," Donna, a slender woman with dark brown hair, said. "Things have actually been pretty great. But the big news is that Steve and I have decided we want to have a baby."

Raised eyebrows and mumbles of "Wow!" came from the other women in the circle.

"I know what you're thinking," Donna continued. I didn't. I had no clue why it was a big deal. "But, my doctor said it's fine and, well, it's time."

"That's great!" Marcia cheered.

"Her ex-husband made her have, like, five abortions," Katie leaned over and conspicuously whispered to me. I couldn't hide my horrified expression.

"Yes, Katie, that's what happened to me. And if Caroline wants to know something, she can ask me." Donna's tone was annoyed.

"Oh, I didn't ask…" I stumbled over my words. I didn't want Donna to think I had somehow solicited the information from Katie. Although she could clearly see I hadn't.

"It's okay, Caroline," Marcia said. "We have an open-book policy here. This is a good and safe place to express any and everything you're going through. You've been through a terribly traumatic experience. We're here to help each other."

I nodded ambiguously. I wasn't making any commitment to spilling my guts to these women.

Sarah talked about having to still see her abuser because her family didn't want to exclude her uncle from family events. She said that even years after finally telling her parents that her uncle sexually abused her from the time she was eight until she was 13, they still questioned if she "remembered things correctly."

At least no one could doubt I had been assaulted.

All in all, it was pretty depressing. Although, as the night went on and they shared parts of their stories, it took the edge off my loneliness. None of them were as horrific as mine, but everyone probably thought that. But none of them had been held captive for 99 days and raped repeatedly so … *I win.*

I pulled up to the house and saw Dad's light on. When I got out of the car, I could see him at his window, but when he saw me looking up, he backed away and turned his light off. So I went inside and climbed the dark stairwell to my room. And thus concluded another day in which I had no idea how to face tomorrow.

Day 265

I took my lunch in my room again. This made 14 days in a row of avoiding my father. I wanted to apologize to him for my behavior, but I was too afraid of the conversation that would follow. Saying I'm sorry would open a gigantic can of worms I wasn't ready for. He would want to know why I freaked out and try to talk about it, which would lead to more freaking out.

It was a really pretty day and I wanted to go see Mom. If I timed it right, I could make it out to the Rourkes' tree where Mom was buried, spend a little bit of time doing the journaling so highly recommended by the survivor's group leader, and then go to the group meeting that night.

No one was more surprised than me that I wanted to go back for a third time to the survivor's group. It turned out to be a group of pretty cool women. Some were older, some younger. Some of them had been recently assaulted, while others were recovering from years of sexual abuse. All of their stories made me sad. I didn't share at either meeting. I just wanted to listen to where everyone else was mentally and emotionally so I didn't feel so alone ... or crazy. I needed to know that freaking out on my dad and holing up in my room for months like a recluse was totally normal. So far no one had expressed those feelings, so I planned to keep going back until I felt validated.

My phone rang, but I ignored it as I always did. Only three people had the number: Dad, Peter, and Officer Moore. Dad and Peter had no reason to call, so there was only one person it could be. If it were really important, like they had caught Mud or something, she would have called Dad when she couldn't reach me. So, as far as I knew, Officer Moore was calling to try and get more information from me. I spent my first weeks home racking my brain and giving them all the painful information I could, but still they came up empty. And since I had no new information to give her, I stopped answering her calls.

I looked at the phone after it stopped ringing and sure enough, it showed a missed call from Officer Moore. I listened to her message. It was the same as all the others. "Hi Caroline. It's Officer Moore. Just calling to check in and see how you're doing. Wanted you to know you weren't forgotten."

Whatever.

I straightened the blanket out next to Mom's headstone and sat down next to her. Coming here never got easier. She would never be any less dead and I could never undo the fact that I hadn't been there when she died. But still I came because being near to her, even like that, felt like the only time I could breathe.

"I'm thinking of getting a job," I said. "I mean, since I can't work on the farm. Well, I guess I technically could, but it'd be weird for everyone. Everybody is nice and cordial when they see me, but no one seems to know how to get back to the way things used to be, especially me. The problem is, I don't have a clue where to look. Can't get a job in town for obvious reasons. So I'd have to go to Stratford or Carson. I don't know."

I lay back on the blanket and looked up at the sky through the edges of the tree and breathed deeply.

"Sorry I don't have more to say today. Not much has changed. I'm another day farther from hell, so there's that. I started going to a support group for survivors of sexual assault. It's better than I thought it would be. I'll keep going, I guess."

I pulled the journal and pen I brought with me out of my purse and opened it. I had only written on a few pages in the last week, but it was a start. None of it had to do with Mud or Owen. Instead I had written down some of my favorite memories of my mom. There were some of my dad, too, since right then it felt like our relationship was as dead as Mom was.

"I don't know how to fix this with Dad," I said. I doodled a flower in the corner of a page filled with memories. "I was really awful, Mom. That damn peanut butter and jelly sandwich. I can barely think about it." I drew a few more petals on the flower. "I know, I know. He had no clue about the sandwich. And yes, I realize I should have just told him. But it's too late for that now."

I heard Mom's voice in my head telling me it's never too late to say you're sorry. It's never too late to explain yourself and make amends. I knew she was right. And in my heart I knew I could trust my dad. But I was so scared of laying it all out on the table with him. I was his baby girl, his only child. He already knew what happened to me. How could he survive my breaking down and vomiting more details at him? No. I wouldn't do it. That's what the support group was for, not that I had shared anything yet. But I would ... probably ... maybe.

"I'll figure it out," I said. "Eventually."

I sat and doodled some more, and then wrote about the time Mom took me to the mall in Stratford to get my ears pierced when I was nine. I had begged her so badly that I forced myself not to cry, even though it hurt like a bitch. I wanted her to see how brave I could be. Some things don't change.

I was the last one to arrive before group started, as I had been the week before. When I arrived early the first time, I discovered everyone else liked to be early so they could chat. I was not a chatterer, so I decided I'd rather arrive just in time and leave immediately after.

"Good evening, ladies," Marcia, the group leader said with a smile. "I hope you've all had a good week. Caroline, it's good to see you back."

"Thanks," I said with a thin-lipped smile. Was she going to acknowledge my attendance every week? That was going to get really old, really fast.

"Would you like to start things off tonight?" she asked.

I shook my head. "I don't think so."

"Everyone shares," Donna said sharply.

"Yeah, well, I don't feel like sharing," I told her.

"She'll share when she's ready," Marcia said.

Donna gave me a disapproving side eye. I crossed my legs and arms protectively. What was her problem? I thought it was supposed to be *support* group. I was not feeling very supported.

Marcia guided the group conversation around the topic of how our abuse affected us in our daily lives. Of the eight of us in the group, I was the newest member. It seemed everyone not only knew each other's stories, but knew each other. They asked questions about jobs and kids, and talked about their struggles moving on after being raped or abused with such ease it unsettled me. I couldn't wrap my brain around it completely.

The group ended and I pulled my purse from under my chair, flinging it over my head and across my body before heading for the door.

Marcia caught me before I could make it half way to my escape. "I really am glad you came back, Caroline."

"Oh, uh, yeah. Me, too," I told her as I walked away.

A cool rush of night air had just hit my face when I heard Donna's voice behind me.

"Why are you here?" she asked.

"What?" I knit my brow together as I turned around.

"Why are you coming to this group?" she challenged again.

"I'm here for the same reason you are," I told her.

"No, you're not. The rest of us, we come here so we can get all that shit out. We come here so we know we're not alone. You sit there with your jaw locked like you've got nothing to say." Donna crossed her arms. The look she gave me was a combination of frustration and compassion. It was weird.

"Maybe I don't have anything to say."

"Then why come?" she asked.

"What is your problem?"

Donna didn't answer, so I turned around and started toward the truck.

"Hey," she called out.

Her tone was much less aggressive, but I didn't stop.

"I'm sorry!"

My mother always said I had a duty to listen to someone when they wanted to apologize, so I turned back around and looked at her expectantly.

"Well?" I said when she stayed silent.

"I've seen girls like you come and go from this group and, well, I don't want to see you get lost," she finally said.

"What does that mean? 'Girls like me'?"

"You come, you listen, you leave. You don't have anyone to talk to so everything you're dealing with stays bottled up," she replied.

"How do you know I don't have anyone to talk to?" I crossed my arms defiantly.

"Even if you have friends you talk to, you don't really have anyone who understands. No one who gets why a song or a color or a time of day is difficult for you." Her eyes were soft as we stood under the bright glow of the parking lot light.

"I don't think any of you could understand what I've been through," I said.

"You think we don't know who you are? Caroline Patterson. The girl who disappeared, showed up three months later. And the fact that you're here only confirms the blanks we all filled in about what happened to you."

I dropped my head. My false sense of anonymity was gone. Donna had seen through me and I could no longer hide.

"And just so you know," she continued. "My ex-husband kept me locked in our bathroom for five days. Came in and out at random times. Raped and sodomized me. It wasn't until my sister started to worry about me that a cop came by. I took a chance and screamed when I heard Reggie talking to him through the bathroom door. It may not have been three months, but yeah, I can understand."

Shaken by her story, I leaned against the car behind me for support. Everyone in the group had given a few details of their stories, but I never dreamed anyone there would have the first clue as to the horror I endured. How could they?

My mind raced. Something in me wanted to spill my story out to Donna. I had already told Dr. Wendy everything, but I delivered that information flatly and with complete disconnection, just like she said. But something was breaking inside me. Maybe that had been Wendy's whole point in sending me to this group. She knew the group would confront me in a way she couldn't, and force me to connect to what happened to me. I couldn't just move on like I had been pretending I could. I searched Donna's waiting eyes and saw what I hadn't realized I needed: a place to lay everything I had been holding in.

I ran my hand down my face and took a deep breath.

"I followed him to his truck because he said he needed a jump."

We stood in that parking lot for the next hour while I told her everything. She didn't say a word, and I barely took a breath. I even told her about Owen. I told her about the things Mud would say to me, and the things he made me say to him. When I finally let go and let the tears fall, Donna stood by me, wrapping her arms around my shoulders, and telling me I was going to be okay.

"No one knows about Owen. Not the police. Not even Dr. Wendy," I told her.

"Why not?"

"He was just as much a prisoner as I was. He never did anything to me. I feel guilty for leaving him behind." I dried my wet face with the sleeves of my hoodie. "You can't tell anyone, Donna. Please."

"Oh, honey. Don't worry, I'm a steel trap," she said.

"Thank you."

We turned and continued deeper into the parking lot toward my car.

"Can I ask you something?" she said. I nodded. "Do you get worried that he'll come look for you?"

"No. The way I figure it, he's probably hiding out. He's gotta know the police are looking for him. Or at least they were. They can't seem to find him," I told her. "What about you? I'm assuming your ex-husband is in jail, but will he get out at some point? Do you think he'll come after you?"

"He's not coming after me, or anyone for that matter."

"How can you be so sure?" No one seemed to know where Mud was, but sometimes I looked over my shoulder just to be safe.

"He already tried that once while he was out on bail," she said.

"What happened?" Curiosity filled me as I wondered how she handled seeing his face again. I didn't know what I'd do if I saw Mud again.

"I shot and killed him." Her answer was delivered as flatly as my entire story had been to Dr. Wendy. Shocked, I covered my mouth.

"Oh, Donna," I said. "That must have been awful."

The corners of her mouth curved with the signs of a slight smile. "Not really," she said. "After I knew he was dead, I felt more peace than I had in seven years we were together. Knowing he was gone from this earth was the best thing that ever happened to me."

"That *would* be the best thing."

Day 35

Click. Squeak.

Mud walked in well after his normal time, as he had the last few days. I hoped he'd arrive earlier, because that would mean he was going to back to work and Owen and I would be safe during the day again. It also meant I could get Owen to let me leave. Until then, the only silver lining—if that's what you could call it—was that I got to lie there for a little while in peace before being treated like an inanimate object once again. I would lie with my head at the opposite end of the bed so I could look out the window. I watched the effect of the wind on the trees, and sometimes a bird would land for a moment on the outside ledge of the window. And, for that moment, I was okay.

Mud being on leave from the factory made everything worse. After the stupidity of saying Owen liked to watch me undress, that became our ritual. Mud came into the room, followed by a sheepish Owen, and demanded I do for him what I had done for Owen. So, I made it up as I went along.

"Up and at 'em, sweetheart!" Mud called. He never called me by my name. That, of course, would humanize me, and he couldn't have that. Mud uncuffed me and hit play on his phone before laying it on the nightstand. It was the same nasty, club thumping, stripper music I would never have pegged a country boy to have, but then again, he did kidnap me, so *never judge a book by its cover* was pretty accurate.

Owen took his usual silent place at the door with his arms folded and his head down. He must have kept Mud in his periphery because he seemed to always look up when Mud looked at him with that huge shit-eating grin.

"Get on with it! I had two bowls of Wheaties this morning so I'm feeling extra good!" Mud laughed.

I took a deep breath, closed my eyes, and started swaying my hips. I had seen enough movies to know how strippers moved. That was all Mud wanted: the movie version of sex.

I hooked my thumbs through my belt loops and rocked my body back and forth. Then I trailed my hands up my sides, over my breasts, and finally through my rat's nest of hair. I brought my hands down and began to unbutton my jeans. I tried not to, but the tears that had been forming in my eyes began to roll down my face. After those first days, I promised myself I wouldn't cry in front of Mud, but I couldn't help it. It was all too much and I didn't know how much longer I would be able to hold on. It didn't faze Mud, but Owen was visibly upset.

I stopped moving and covered my face. Mud grabbed me by the arm, forcing my hands down, and slapped me. "Who said you could stop?"

"That's ... that's enough," Owen said. He pushed off the doorframe and shoved in front of Mud, turning the music off.

"What the fuck? I straightened her out. It was just about to get good!" Mud declared.

Owen looked at me and I hoped with everything in me that he was about to tell Mud to go to hell and to let me go. That the last few days of watching Mud denigrate me further had sparked a new strength in him to fight for me.

No such luck.

"I don't like it like that," Owen began. "I don't like that music."

"Are you telling me you like it all soft and sweet and shit?" Mud laughed and shook his head. "Well why didn't you say so? We can make her do whatever we want! I'll change up the playlist, brother!"

Mud reached for his phone but Owen stopped him.

"No, no music."

Mud scrunched his eyebrows together and huffed. "Whatever floats your boat. All right, sweetheart. Owen says no music. Get back to it."

When I didn't move, Mud raised his hand to hit me again.

"No!" Owen said, stopping Mud's arm in midair. It was clear from the confused expression on Mud's face that Owen had never done anything like that before. It scared me because I didn't know how angry it would make Mud. "She's mine."

My eyes widened, but not as wide as Mud's. Owen released his arm and Mud turned to face him. He surveyed his younger brother with narrowed eyes.

"You said she was a gift for me," Owen told him. "I ... I don't want to share her anymore."

My heart pounded so strong and loud I was certain they could both hear me. This was it. Owen was taking ownership of me, which meant he could do whatever he wanted with me, including letting me go. Excitement and fear filled me. What was Mud going to do?

Mud's perturbed expression softened. He leaned into his brother, speaking softly.

"You know I don't got another way to get it," he said. What did that mean? I had prayed to God Mud wasn't married, but I was sure plenty of women nearby would do just about anything for the right amount.

"I know," Owen replied. "But I been thinkin' and if she's really a gift to me then I get to say what happens with her."

Yes! This is it!

"What are you sayin'?" Mud asked.

"I'm sayin'," Owen began hesitantly. I'd never seen him so bold with his brother before. "I'm sayin' that you only get her once a day."

What? NO! This is the part where you tell Mud to go to hell! Where you tell him that if I'm really your gift then you get to decide what happens to me, and you decide that I get to go home! Tell him, Owen!

Mud stepped back, shocked at his brother's assertiveness. He thought for a moment before speaking. My eyes darted between the two of them. For as confident as Owen had just been, he still looked like a scared little boy.

"You know what?" Mud started. "You're right. I brought her here for you." Owen's tense body relaxed. "But if I only get her once a day, then I want it now."

Mud turned his attention my way, closing the small gap between us with a forceful stride. He grabbed my shirt and ripped it open, scattering buttons across the floor. Then he tossed me onto the bed. I tried to fight, but the back of his right hand across my face quickly reminded me it was pointless. He stripped my jeans and panties from me and slammed into me with more force than he ever had.

Tears gushed from my eyes. I didn't even try to stop them. I knew it got him even more excited, but I didn't care anymore. I just wanted it to be over. I just wanted it to all be over. I lay there with my head turned to the side, letting the deluge of tears flow.

Owen looked at me with sadness. He had a chance to save me and he didn't take it. Instead, he left me in that room while his brother raped me again and again.

Day 270

"Thanks for meeting me," I said to Donna as we sat down at a diner close to the hospital. Anderson's was closer for both of us, but I can never go back there.

"Sure," she said. "Sorry if I was hard on you the other day."

"It's okay. I guess I needed it. I feel like I'm thinking clearly for the first time."

The waitress approached and handed us to menus. "Hey, I'm Dara. I'll be taking care of you today. Can I get you something to drink?" she asked with a bright smile.

"I'll just have a Coke," Donna told her.

"Same here," I said.

"Great. I'll be back in a few to get your order." Dara walked off happily to get our drinks. We perused the menus for a few minutes, making our decisions before laying them on the table.

"So?" Donna looked at me with anticipation, her eyebrows almost reaching her hairline.

I took a breath and asked what had been on my mind.

"How did you get through every day? I wake up and have no idea what I'm doing," I blurt out just as Dara returns with our drinks. She doesn't bat an eye. I'm sure she's heard crazier things come from these tables.

"Here you go," Dara says as she places our drinks on the table in front of us. "What can I get you?"

"I'll have the turkey club with fries," Donna says.

"And I'll have the grown-up grilled cheese, also with fries. Thanks." I pick up both menus and hand them to Dara.

"Got it. I'll put these right in. Just let me know if you need anything in the meantime." Dara smiled and left us to continue our conversation.

"Well," Donna began. "That's a hard thing to answer. At first it was extremely difficult. My ex had been arrested but the lovely court system set his bail at ten grand. His parents came to his rescue and got him out the next day. I spent days looking over my shoulder. Now, that's something you don't have to worry about."

"That's true. I'm not worried that he's coming after me. It's all the other stuff I can't seem to get a hold of," I said. "Before I left, I had been taking care of my mom. Her cancer had gotten worse and she needed my help all the time. But before that, I worked on our cattle farm almost every day. It's a family business, so that was my plan. I finished school and was going to spend my life working for my dad."

Dara arrived with our lunches and set them down in front of us. She asked if we needed anything, and then told us to enjoy when we said we were all set.

"So why can't you do that?" Donna dipped a fry in ketchup and ate it.

"It's complicated." I pulled my sandwich apart and began salivating at the gooey threads of cheese.

"Feeling like a leper is not complicated." Donna looked at me knowingly.

"Oh my God! Yes! That's *exactly* how I feel!" I said excitedly.

"We all feel that way. We're the ones who were violated and yet somehow we're the ones no one can look in the eye. Like we did something wrong." Donna rolled her eyes. "What people don't realize is that we *need* them to look us in the eye so we can start rebuild the trust we lost with humanity at the hands of our rapists."

"Dad … Peter … for some reason they don't know what to say to me. Do they think I want to sit around and chat about that time? No! I just want to talk to Peter about regular things the way we used to. And I want my Dad to have more to say than how accomplished he feels about his day." I sighed. "But I'm not helping the situation. I close myself off in my room all day, or I just leave and spend the day at my mother's grave. I'm frustrated and sad that they don't talk to me, but I don't know what to say either."

"I get it," Donna said simply. "Everyone needs time. And when you're ready, you'll be able to teach them how to interact with you again. But you've all got to be patient with each other. Trust me."

"So? How did you get through it?" I reiterated my question.

Donna shook her head. "What I've learned in the last eight years is that talking about it is your best first step. But the thing that got me through was something my grandma used to say: *There is no force more powerful than a woman determined to rise.* And I was determined to rise up from the ashes."

"Reggie being dead was probably a huge help, too," I said in between bites.

"Reggie being dead just meant I didn't have to look over my shoulder. It meant I never had to fear for any other women out there. But it didn't make what happened go away. I had a lot of nightmares. And when I first started dating my husband, it took a *long* time before I could let him do more than hold my hand."

"I have nightmares, too. Sometimes they're not about Mud. Sometimes they're about Owen," I said. "I get concerned that Mud did something terrible to him after he let me go."

"That's not on you. They both made their choices. Your focus was your survival at any cost." Donna looked at me sternly. She didn't want me carrying guilt for any part of my experience.

I nodded. "That's true."

We sat in silence for a few minutes, eating our lunch, while I contemplated everything Donna had said. I had wasted nine months thinking that once Mud was caught and brought to justice, I'd be able to move on with my life. I couldn't waste any more time. It would have to be enough to know that Officer Moore was still doing everything she could to investigate and find Mud.

"So," I finally said. I decided to change the subject to something that had nothing to do with either of our trauma … something that could only be filled with joy. "Tell me about your baby plans!"

Day 275

It turns out spilling my guts to Donna was better than all the therapy I had with Dr. Wendy. No offense to Dr. Wendy. Donna and I texted almost every day and had a few conversations that went late into the night. She was so right. Having someone who understood what I went through helped more than I realized. Still, it had been a while and so, at her request, I planned to check in with Wendy. It'd also been quite some time since I touched base with Office Moore, so stopped by the Pinewood police station before my appointment.

I walked through the front door and watched as a few eyebrows rose at the sight of me. Evidence that my absence had been noted and my arrival was a surprise.

From across the room filled with desks positioned in sets of two, back to back, Office Moore called my name. She walked swiftly as she met me where I stood.

"Caroline. It's so good to see you," she smiled. "Is everything okay?"

"Yeah, everything's good. I just wanted to touch base," I told her.

"Great! Follow me and we'll chat."

I followed her to the back of the room and then down a short hallway to an interrogation room. I checked myself briefly in the two-way mirror as I walked in. I looked tired. I was 18 years old and I looked 40. I suppose not sleeping well for nine months will do that to you, among other things.

"I've actually been meaning to call you this week," Officer Moore said as she closed the door behind her.

"Oh yeah?" I said. Five months ago I would have been excited and assumed she had news about my case, but so far she'd only called to check on me and ask if I'd remembered anything new.

"Yes," she answered. "But why don't you go first. You took the time to come all the way over here to see me."

"Oh, well ... I guess part of me wanted to apologize. It might seem like I've given up, but I haven't. I mean, I know I don't follow up like I used to and it's definitely taking a lot more time than I thought it would but, I want you to know I trust you. You're working my case with all the information and, well ... you'll get him." I nodded with a flat smile, trying to convey my belief in the system and convince myself I believed what I'd just said.

"That's very kind of you, Caroline," Officer Moor said. Her expression turned somber. "But it makes what I have to tell you even harder. My boss has slowly been moving your case to the back burner. We've followed every lead and exhausted every resource we had, but we've still come up empty." She swallowed hard, buying herself a single moment before continuing. "Until we get new lead, your case goes on the unsolved stack."

I listened to the words coming from her, but I had a hard time processing what she said. Was she abandoning my case?

"What does that mean?" I asked. I felt my face squish together in confusion.

"It means Officer Day and I can't work your case unless a brand new lead comes in. Your file won't be closed, but it'll be classified as unsolved."

I paced the room for a solid minute, running through the last six months in my mind and reviewing every sordid detail of my experience. I had told them everything. Everything except about Owen's existence. But there was no way I could tell them about him. I had planned to deny knowing about Owen when they caught Mud. After everything Owen had done for me, I wouldn't let him be lumped in with that douchebag brother of his.

"How?" I asked.

"How what?"

"How haven't you found him yet?" I nearly shouted. Officer Moore looked stunned. It was a question I had never posed. And considering the speech I had just given about trusting that they'd find him one day, a little out of nowhere.

"I understand this is upsetting for you, Caroline."

"You understand shit! But what I don't understand is how can you possibly have searched a 10-mile radius from where I was picked up and not found him or the house. How many Muds can there be in Pollack County?"

"That's just it!" She raised her volume to match mine. "We can't find anyone named Mud."

"What? That's impossible."

She sighed. "We searched those woods and the surrounding towns for well over a month. There are plenty of guys named Bud and Buddy, but no one named Mud. And the house ... practically everyone out there has an old cottage behind their house. And, quite frankly, most of them look the same from the outside."

"You have to go in! You have to see the room with the lock and bed and the shower and the…"

"We can't just search houses, Caroline. Without probable cause, we can't force our way in."

"What about the description I gave you? Can't you go on that?" I asked.

"Tall, dark hair, rough around the edges? You described half the men in every factory town around here. Are you sure he didn't have any distinguishing marks?" Officer Moore had asked me that question a hundred times, and a hundred times I gave her the same answer.

"No. No distinguishing marks. If he did, I would have told you." I put my hands on my hips and paced the room. "What about the truck? Didn't Meg give you a description of the truck?" This was a question I had asked Officer Moore a hundred time and a hundred times she told me the same thing.

"All Meg said was that it was a dark green truck. She didn't get a tag number. Do you know how many green trucks are in that ten-mile radius? The ones we found weren't linked to anyone who matched Mud's description. And those that were close to his description all had airtight alibis for the day you were taken." Officer Moore closed the distance between us and took me by my shoulders. "I am not giving up. As soon as we have a new lead, I'll be the first one out there. Next to you, no one wants to take this guy down more than me."

I sat in Dr. Wendy's waiting room with Office Moore's words echoing in my head. I wondered how long she had been sitting on the whole "your file is being classified as unsolved." All that time I thought they had been doing something. Turns out they were just procrastinating in telling me I was shit out of luck in ever seeing my rapist brought to justice.

Wendy appeared at the door and greeted me. "Hi Caroline. I'm glad you were able to make the time to check in."

"Sure," I said as we took our usual places.

"Are you okay?" she asked.

"That's not very therapeutic of you," I joked.

"Well, sometimes 'are you okay' is the best I've got." She chuckled. "So ... are you?"

How was I to put into words that every hope I had of closure had been erased?

"I just came from the police station," I said.

"Didn't get the news you hoped for?"

"Nope. In fact, I got the opposite. They're reclassifying my file to 'unsolved.'"

Wendy took a deep breath through her nose and pressed her lips together. "That sucks."

I nodded. "Yep."

"So, you're here. Let's talk about it."

"There's nothing to talk about. It sucks. It's not like I can do anything about it. I can't force them to go back out and find the same nothing they found months ago. They can't search every house in the area because they don't have probable cause. And—here's my favorite part—they can't find anyone named Mud in a 10-mile radius of where I was picked up. So, what am I gonna do?" I crossed my arms in what must have looked like a show of aggravation to Wendy. In reality, I was doing my best to stay closed off enough so as to not mention Owen.

"How's this for a therapeutic question: how does it make you feel that they're reclassifying your case as unsolved?" Wendy asked.

"Well, I kind of yelled at Officer Moore," I told her. Wendy's eyebrows shot up.

"That's great!"

"Why is that great?"

"Because you're finally expressing some anger," she said. "I haven't been able to put my finger on why, but you've been holding back. Like you're refusing to acknowledge your anger."

"I'm not holding anything back," I lied.

"Okay," Wendy said, attempting to pacify me.

"I'm not holding anything back!" I reiterated. "I'm angry."

"I said okay, Caroline."

"Yeah, but I can tell you don't believe me."

"Is it important to you that I believe you?" She asked, cocking her head to the side in that therapisty way.

"What do you want me to do?" I raised my voice like I had at Officer Moore.

"I want you to express your anger in a way that is most authentic to you. Whether that means screaming inarticulately into a pillow or crying or talking it out using every expletive in the book, that's up to you. But you can't rely on the police to bring you closure. Closure is about how *you* decide the story ends. The reality is they may never catch him. And you have to find a way to accept that. Along the path to acceptance there are several stops. One of those stops is anger."

She was right. Officer Moore had put the brakes on investigating my case, which meant Mud would never be caught. There was nothing I could do. I wanted closure, like Wendy said, but I didn't know how to get it. I would never be handed the same prime opportunity Donna had to end her ordeal and determine her own closure.

But ... that the opportunity wouldn't be handed to me didn't mean I couldn't create it.

And just like that, the wheels started turning in my head like they never had before. The unthinkable stormed through my brain in ways that seemed quite reasonable. A plan, one as insane as they come, formed in my mind with clarity. I didn't care how long it took. I would find Mud myself and kill him.

"Okay. How's this for authentic anger: I want him dead."

Day 50

Squeak. Tap. Click.

God, I hated those sounds.

I used to love them because it meant Mud was finished with me until he got home from work at night. It started the clock ticking on the time I had to breathe, to hope. But there was no more hope. Owen's limits on Mud had reduced the number of times per day he could rape me, which was especially good on the weekends when Mud had been in my room four or five times a day. But since he only got one shot, he became more aggressive. Angrier. He used to hit me once in a while, but he did it almost every time now. He graduated to choking me a few times as well.

The worst part was that I heard those sounds more since Owen stopped coming to read with me. Instead of coming and staying with me, he dropped food off like a warden and left, locking the door behind him.

Mud raped me.

Squeak. Tap. Click.

Owen brought me breakfast.

Squeak. Tap. Click.

Owen brought me lunch.

Squeak. Tap. Click.

Owen brought me a snack.

Squeak. Tap. Click.

Owen brought me dinner.

Squeak. Tap. Click.

And an extra *squeak, tap, click* on days when I got to shower.

I tried to talk to Owen; tried to tell him that I wasn't mad, even though I hated him. I thought I hated him most for not letting me go. But as the days went by, I began to hate him for leaving me alone. It may have been some jacked up version of Stockholm Syndrome, but I didn't care. I began to miss Owen's company. He was all I had. The only thing that wasn't tearing me apart. And when it came down to it, we were both Mud's prisoners.

I wondered if he went anywhere in between bringing me food, or if he sat sadly in the living room, waiting until time to feed me. Sometimes I heard Mud yell at him in the evening after dinner. I couldn't be sure, but it sounded like Mud was slurring his words. He begged Owen to change his mind on the limits, but Owen always said no. It was hard to believe, but Mud actually respected Owen's rules, so at least I had that.

Tap. Squeak.

The door opened and Owen walked in with a plate of cheese toast and a glass of milk. He set it on the table and turned to leave. My approach of telling him I wasn't mad hadn't worked, so it was time to try something new.

"Owen, are you mad at me?" I asked. Previously when I spoke to him he ignored me and left the room. This questioned stopped him cold.

He turned around. "I'm not mad at you, Caroline." He looked shocked.

"Then why haven't you been back to read with me? Why are you leaving me all alone?"

He thought for a moment before he answered. "Cuz I wish I was smart enough to know what to do."

"You are smart. You're very smart. Because of your decision, Mud only comes to me once a day," I said. "I appreciate that. Thank you."

"You're welcome," he said. "You really think I'm smart?"

This would be the part in the movie where the girl would lie to her captor to butter him up so she could convince him to let her go. But I wasn't lying to Owen.

"Yes, I do. Look how far you've come in your reading in just a little while. When we first started reading together, you barely knew anything," I said. "I'm really proud of you."

Owen's face lit up and his eyes were brighter. I was sure he'd never heard anyone tell him they were proud of him. That broke what was left my heart.

He left the room and returned quickly, a book in his hand. "*The Wizard of Oz?*"

I drew in a cleansing breath and reached my hand out. "This is one of my favorites."

I ate my toast and we took turns reading. He stumbled over a few words we had worked hard to conquer before, but he picked it back up pretty quickly. Within a few hours we had made it half way through the book.

"This is even better than the movie!" he said.

"The book is always better than the movie!" I said and, forgetting where I was, I laughed.

Owen picked up my lunch dishes and moved toward the door.

"Owen," I said softly. "My mom still needs me."

He dropped his head. "I know. And I'm sorry. But I can't let you go right now."

"Why not?" I scooted to the end of the bed eager for him to hear me and change his mind. "You were ready to let me go before."

"I know. But Mud's real mad at me since I said he could only come see you once a day. If I let you go, he'll be even madder. I don't like it when Mud's real mad."

"What would happen if Mud got madder?" I asked. "Would he hurt you?"

Owen's eyes got big. "Oh, no ma'am! Mud's never hurt me before. He loves me and he protects me. But sometimes, if I do something I'm not supposed to do, he takes my Hot Wheels away."

It was so much worse than I thought. Owen, whose young mind was trapped in grown man's body, collected cars. And the thing he feared most was his brother taking his toys away from him.

"Well, that seems pretty mean," I said. What else could I say? "But I can understand why you wouldn't want to make Mud mad." Owen nodded.

That's when I found myself in the strangest place of all: feeling sorrier for Owen than I did myself.

Day 276

It was late when I got home after my appointment with Dr. Wendy. I had to stop by Mom's grave and explain myself. I told her that the best-case scenario would leave Mud dead and me moving on with my life. Closure. The worst case? I'd see her soon.

The wheels in my head hadn't stopped turning since that moment in Dr. Wendy's office. I had to come up with a solid plan that would pay off. I spent the evening with an old fashioned map laid out in front of me on my bed. I couldn't get enough perspective with the one I had pulled up online. I circled the spot where I had been found and then pulled out a compass and drew my own 10-mile radius. When I was done, I chuckled at the fact that I actually had a map and a compass. We had all sorts of traditional learning tools from when Mom homeschooled me. Those were the best years of my life, and I was determined to get them back.

I tossed a few things into a backpack and grabbed my phone, shoving it in my back pocket. It was just after ten in the morning and Dad had long since been out in the field or the barn. I made my way into his bedroom and found the Glock he kept under his t-shirts in his dresser. It was fully loaded, as always.

I hopped in the truck and drove to the slaughter building to look for Dad and Peter. I planned on telling them I was going to take a drive out to Gramma and Grandpa Patterson's lake house and stay for a few nights, so I wanted to say goodbye. When I got to the building, I didn't see them, but I did see Peter's .22-caliber rifle. I grabbed it quickly and laid it on the floor of the truck. With any luck, he wouldn't notice it missing anytime soon. When I returned, Dad and Peter were entering the building from the far end.

"Hi," I said as I met them where they had stopped. They were going over something on a clipboard and hadn't seen me.

"Oh, Caroline," Dad said, taken aback. "I didn't see you. You're … here. You haven't been out here in ages. Is everything okay? Are you okay?" He looked concerned. If he only knew what I was about to embark on. I had to succeed at my mission of finding and ending Mud. My sanity depended on it. But he could turn the tables on me and I would end up dead. I hated the idea of leaving Dad to bury another loved one, but I was already dead inside. My only hope of revival was eliminating Mud from this earth.

"Sorry. Didn't mean to startle you," I said with a weak smile. "I wanted to tell you I'm going to be gone for a couple of nights. I'm going to head up to the lake house. Dr. Wendy wants me to do all this journaling stuff and I figured it'd be a good place to clear my head."

"Oh man! I haven't been out there in ages," Peter said with a smile. Seeing him smile in my direction again gave me hope that one day we'd be back to normal. It'd been a long time, and I missed it more than I realized.

"I think that's a great idea." Dad smiled hopefully. After I blew up at him, things had been even tenser than when I first came home. I'm sure he was all for me doing anything to help us get back to normal. Well, anything but murdering my rapist.

"Great! I'm just going to stop by the bank and take some cash out for gas and to pick up some food, and then I'll be on my way," I told them. I turned and started back the way I came but stopped and turned back around after only a few steps. "Hey, Dad?" He lifted his chin and raised his eyebrows in anticipation of what I was about to say. "I love you."

Dad smiled widely while his eyes became glassy. "I love you, too, sweetheart."

I turned to go back to the car and had only taken a few steps when Peter said my name and grabbed my elbow.

"Hey, Caroline," he said. I turned and raised my eyebrows to ask him what he wanted. "I, well, I know things haven't been the same between us since you got home. I just wanted to say I'm sorry."

"Why are you sorry, Peter?" I asked.

"Because it's my fault."

"We've been over that—"

"No, not that. I mean, yes, I still feel some guilt there, but that's not what I'm talking about. I should have been more attentive to you. I honestly didn't know what to say or do. You tried so hard to get things to go back to normal, and I abandoned you." His eyes turned red and watery. He was right. I had tried and he had ignored me. "When you get back from the lake house, maybe we can start over again?"

I sighed with relief. The timing of his sentiment was perfect. When I got back, I'd have closure and be in a much better place myself to reconnect to the life I once had.

"I think that's a great idea, Peter," I said. "When I get back, I have a feeling I'm going to have a whole new outlook on life." Peter and I mirrored big smiles at one another.

With that, I made my way back to the other end of the building. I was about to step into the sunshine when something caught my eye. There, on a table of tools and gadgets, was a cap bolt gun. The same one Peter had taken to Renfrow's to be repaired the day Mud stole me.

No. No, Caroline. Taking a cap bolt gun to Mud's head would be too much, I told myself. *Was it too much for Mud to rape and beat me every day for over three months?*

One foul deed deserved another.

I looked to be sure Dad and Peter weren't watching, picked up the cap bolt gun, and made a beeline for the truck. I took a deep breath, put the truck in gear, and started on my mission to finally find closure.

After a quick stop at the bank, I filled the truck up with gas and equipped myself with an assortment of unhealthy snacks and drinks. The first stop on my journey was the Macon County Hospital two hours away, so I settled in for the drive.

Two hours, three bags of chips, and two sodas later, I pulled into the hospital parking lot to get my bearings. I considered going inside to say thank you to the nurses who had helped me, especially Nurse

MaryKay, but I couldn't delay my task any longer. The sooner I made it to Saw Mill Road, the closer I would be to finding Mud.

I laid the map on the hood of the car and followed the already highlighted line from the hospital to Saw Mill Road. Then I pulled out my phone and set the destination in my maps app. One hour and 15 minutes.

Only then I realized the time frame of my abduction. After Mud knocked me out, I lay unconscious in the bed of his truck for at least three hours.

The fire of my revenge fully engaged, I folded the map, got back in the truck, and hit the road. There would be no major highways on this road trip. There were none around these parts. But there would be a lot of two lane roads and highway bypasses with beautiful scenery, and I would enjoy every piece of it.

I easily cut 15 minutes off the drive time to my destination. My lead foot was anxious. I stopped my car at a T-junction and stared at the street sign for what seemed like eternity. Saw Mill Road. This was it. The real beginning of everything. I swallowed hard and turned left.

It was a normal road; not anything I remembered as being distinct. But as I drove further some things seemed to feel familiar. There was a freshly placed wreath honoring someone who had died, probably in an accident at that spot. I remembered seeing one as I leaned my head against the window the day I was picked up. And then there were huge logs where trees had fallen across the road and locals had chain sawed them apart and left them.

But my heart stopped when I saw the abandoned general store where the kindly trucker had picked me up.

I pulled over to the side of the road, got out, and crossed the street. My heart started to race as I approached the building. I remembered how it smelled: old and musty. And even though I was wearing shoes this time, the ground beneath my feet somehow felt familiar.

I looked out in both directions. The road curved and disappeared behind the woods on both sides. What was I doing? This wasn't me. Hot tears rolled down my face as my temperature began to rise. The skin from my neck to my ears was warm to the touch, and likely flushed. No. This wasn't me. But I wasn't me anymore. Mud took that girl away, but I was about to get her back.

I marched back to the car and pulled the map out, finding my location. If I continued down Saw Mill Road, I'd run straight into the town of Jubilee. That would be where I started looking. So I pulled my hair into a ponytail and fixed my favorite ball cap to my head, threading my hair through the hole in the back, and turned the key in the ignition.

As I pulled back on to the road, something Donna said to me echoed in my mind: There is no force more powerful than a woman determined to rise. And rise I would.

I drove another thirty minutes down the winding road and passed a sign welcoming me to Jubilee before I came to the end and faced the choice of turning left or right. I had hoped to get a sense of where I had emerged from the woods that day but I couldn't remember if I had crossed the road and then came upon the abandoned general store, or if I had been on that side of the road the whole time. That frustrated me more than anything. It meant that whichever direction I turned was a crapshoot, a 50/50 chance of getting it right. A wrong turn would mean I'd be wasting time in a town with no chance of finding Mud.

I blew out a gust of air and turned left. It was 20 minutes down the two-lane road before I hit town.

How ironic if I had been held captive in a town called Jubilee.

Jubilee appeared bigger than Pinewood but still small enough to be the kind of place where everyone knew everyone. At least, that was my hope. The town had two wide lanes running through it with parking on either side for the businesses that lined the street. With wooden buildings and slatted wood overhangs, it was something out of an old western.

I pulled into a parking space in front of a place called Toad in the Hole. It looked a lot like Anderson's, a place likely frequented by the residents of Jubilee. It seemed like a good place to start digging. And it was after 1:00, so I figured I'd get something to eat while I was at it.

The bell above the door rang out as I entered the restaurant. The place was about a third full of patrons. Most of the men dressed in rugged jeans, button down shirts to protect them from the sun, baseball hats, and work boots.

A woman's voice called out from the back, telling me to sit anywhere I wanted and that she'd be right with me. I chose a seat at the end of the counter and picked up the menu that was shoved between condiment bottles and salt and pepper shakers. I was deciding between the patty melt and meatloaf sandwich when a guy at the other end of the counter left his friend and sat next to me.

"Hey," he said.

"Hi." I didn't look up from the menu in hopes that he'd get the idea and leave me alone.

"What's your name?"

"None of your business," I told him.

"That's not very nice of you. C'mon. Tell me your name," he reiterated. I continued ignoring him. "You could at least smile for me."

Seriously? Why do guys always want women to smile? His proximity to me made the hair on the back of my neck stand up. Instinctively I wanted to punch him in the nuts, but I opted for not drawing too much attention to myself.

"I'm just passing through, so why don't you leave me alone," I told him.

"Just passing through, huh?" He leaned in closer. "Even better."

"She said to leave her alone, Eugene!" A woman appeared from the kitchen with a scowl on her face and a tone that said she meant business. She looked to be in her late 60's, thin with graying blonde hair.

"I'm just havin' fun with her, Ruth," Eugene replied.

"Well I've got a shotgun back here and I'm about to have fun shootin' your balls off. Now back up offa her!" Ruth stepped forward and put her palms on the counter and her face in Eugene's.

"Damn! Why you gotta get all rough like that!" Eugene returned to his seat and sulked like a little boy.

"You all right, sweetie?" Ruth asked.

"Yes. I'm fine." My tone was short.

"What's your name?" she asked while grabbing a glass and filling it with ice and water from a pitcher. I didn't answer. "Well la-dee-da! Aren't you little miss independent! I'll leave you to the menu then."

Ruth walked around the counter and checked on customers, refilling waters and clearing a few plates. When she returned, I corrected my behavior, not only because it was the polite thing to do, but because I was not going to get anywhere by alienating someone who might be able to help. Ruth had already proven herself to be tough as well as sympathetic to a girl traveling alone, and her position at the restaurant meant that she likely knew most everyone in town. She'd be my best first resource.

"Hey, I'm sorry I was rude," I told her. "Just shaken from Eugene over there."

"Don't sweat it, darlin'! Like water off a duck's back!" She smiled and took out a notepad from her pocket. "What'll ya have?"

"I think I'm going to have the patty melt and a Coke." I nodded and slid the menu back where I got it.

"Good choice." Ruth wrote it down and slid the paper through the window to the kitchen before turning back to you. "So … how 'bout that name?"

"Mary," I said. "Mary Offerman." My mother's name would do just fine as my alias.

"Well, Mary, I'm Ruth and welcome to my place." A big smile spread across Ruth's face as she extended her hand. I reached across the counter, shook her hand, and tried to paint on a comparable smile. "Heard you say you were just passing through. Where you on your way to?"

"Not sure," I told her. "I'm looking for someone."

"Well, if they're in Jubilee, you'll find 'em. A postage stamp has more square feet than this town. This person gotta name?" she asked.

I unrolled the silverware from my napkin and placed them neatly on the counter before laying the napkin on my lap.

"That's the hard part. I only have a first name."

"How the hell did you find yourself looking for someone you only have the first name of?" Ruth leaned against the workstation behind her.

"I don't want to be rude, but ... it's kinda personal," I said.

Ruth nodded and gave me a crooked smile. "All right, I hear ya," she said. "We all got our secrets."

"Thanks for understanding. So, is there any chance you think you might be able to help me? I mean, you seem like the kind of person who knows *everyone*." I put on a sugary sweet tone to butter her up.

"I see what you're doing ... and I'm still gonna help you!" Ruth pushed off the back workstation and pulled a big canister of salt from below the counter. She gathered the saltshakers along the counter and began refilling or topping them off while we talked. "So who are we looking for?"

I took a deep breath. What if she knew Mud? What if she knew him and considered him a pillar of the community? If she knew him, she'd want to know why I was looking for him. I certainly couldn't tell her he had held me captive for 99 days and I was there to exact my revenge.

"That's kinda personal, too."

She cocked her head to the side and examined my face. "All right, little miss tight-lipped. I get it. A lot of the guys at the factory on this side of town, I know them more by face than by name. Can you tell me what he looks like?" she asked.

"Yeah. He's a little over six feet, dark brown hair, brown eyes, good-looking but a little rough around the edges. He might have a limp."

Ruth laughed. "Honey! You just described almost every guy at that factory!"

"Even the limp?" I questioned.

"Darlin'! That factory is filled with clumsy lugs!"

"Perfect." Disappointment coated my tone.

"Aww, honey, don't be too discouraged. You're welcome to hang out here tomorrow and see if he's with the guys who come in for lunch," she offered.

"They come in lunch? Every day?" My hope revived.

"A lot of them do. I offer a five-dollar lunch special just for the factory guys. They come in around noon, so if you want to come back then…"

"Order up!" a man's voice shouted from the kitchen as my patty melt appeared in the window.

Ruth placed my lunch in front of me. "Here you go, honey. Enjoy!"

I had missed the lunch crowd by minutes. But at least I had a lead. I would definitely be back the next day to see if Mud was among the lunch patrons. Suddenly starving, I took a big bite of my sandwich.

Yes, I'd be back tomorrow for Mud, and most definitely for another patty melt.

Day 60

As the days went by, Owen become stronger. He demanded that Mud release me to shower every day. It meant that Mud came to me a little earlier each day, but the sooner he was there, the sooner he left. Owen had already released me once while Mud wasn't there, so the key to the handcuffs was in the house somewhere. I didn't understand why he allowed Mud to be its keeper, but I had to continue to working on Owen to let me go.

Owen also told Mud to acquire a TV/VCR for me. I assumed that, along with his children's books, Owen still had a collection of movies from when he was little. I could only imagine what they were, but at least it would add some variety to our day.

"Why the hell does she need that?" Mud demanded.

"I ain't gonna be in there all day. If she's gonna stay, I won't hurt nothin' for her to have something to watch," Owen told him.

I had dressed and was drying my hair with the towel when Mud returned to reattach me to the bed. We never spoke, and he never looked me in the eye, even though I tried hard to make him. If he'd just look at me, then he'd see me as a human being and not a toy.

"Mud," I called as he walked away. I hated calling him by his name when what I really wanted to call him was douche bag, asshole, or monster. "I want to go home."

He stopped in his tracks and turned around, finally looking me in the eye. He took three steps toward me and pointed his thick finger at me.

"You ain't goin' nowhere."

I lowered my head and regretted ever wanting to look him in the eyes. When I did, it was scarier than I had expected. They were dark and cold, and something demonic swirled in them.

He left and slammed the door behind him.

Squeak. Tap. Click.

Mud began yelling at Owen almost immediately.

"This ain't workin'!" he said to Owen. "I brought her here and now I hardly get to use her. And since I ain't in there enough for her to know her place, she got it in her head to tell me she wants to leave. This was *not* what I had in mind!"

After a moment of silence, Owen replied. I knew he was thinking of what he should say. It took him longer to formulate his thoughts, and he didn't want to anger Mud any more than he already was.

Owen wasn't going to raise his voice, so I moved to the door and pressed my ear against it so I could hear what he said.

"Well," Owen began. "Maybe she can go home."

"What?" Mud's voice reverberated down the hall and hit the door like wave.

"We've had our fun," Owen said.

"You cut off my fun! And you know I ain't gettin' it anywhere else."

"I didn't cut you off, Mud. I just … just…" Owen had trouble finding the words he needed.

"Just, just, just … spit it out, dammit!"

I covered my mouth at Mud's cruelty. This was the loving brother Owen had said *loved* and *protected* him? I couldn't believe it was a one-time mistake on Mud's part, that he only made fun of his challenged brother in the heat of their argument. No. His mocking spoke to the blackness of Mud's heart. The question was, could I convince Owen of that darkness?

"I told you, Mud. I just wanted her more to myself," Owen finally said.

"Fine!" Footsteps stormed in my direction, causing me to scurry back to the bed. "I gotta get to work. Don't do anything stupid while I'm gone!" The door to the house opened and closed with a fury, shaking the walls.

I watched the bedroom door, waiting for Owen. He was usually there with my breakfast a few minutes after Mud left, but at least twice that much time passed. I wondered if Owen was angry with me for telling Mud I wanted to leave. Did he blame me for their argument? I drummed my fingers across my left hand and waited.

Tap. Squeak.

Owen appeared with a plate of food that smelled nothing like toast and cheese. As he set the dish down next to me, I saw the most delicious-looking cheese omelet. He placed the glass of milk next to the dish and stepped back.

"What's this?" I asked.

"I'm sorry Mud was rude to you," he said.

I raised my eyebrows in shock. Mud's rudeness to me was the least of my worries, and Owen was sorry about that? How about "I'm sorry my brother brutally rapes you"?

"Don't be sorry, Owen. Mud is responsible for his own actions." I picked up the plate and realized there was no fork. "Um..."

Owen pulled a fork from his back pocket and eyed it cautiously.

"Mud says I'm not supposed to give you a fork or knife cuz you might try to hurt me and escape."

"I would never hurt you, Owen."

He twisted the utensil around in his hand a few times before giving it to me. Our hands touched when I took it from him and I watched the effect a gentle touch had on him: a sudden intake of air, wider eyes, and a soft smile. My heart broke that something so simple could mean so much.

"This is really good, Owen. Where'd you learn to cook?" I asked. I scarfed down another few bites and then took a long sip of milk.

"I watch a lot of cooking shows," he said with an embarrassed smile. "There's nothing else worth watching during the day. Just a bunch of soap operas and game shows."

"Yeah, I see your point." I finished the first hot breakfast I'd had in two months with a satisfied sigh. "You can make me an omelet anytime!"

Owen returned from taking my dishes with two VHS tapes. The cardboard sleeves were worn and tattered.

"Wanna watch a movie?" Owen asked. His face was bright and excited, like I was a friend over for a play date.

"Sure," I answered. "What are my choices?"

Owen laid the two movies on the bed before me. "*The Lion King* or *The Little Mermaid*."

"Hmmm ... that's a tough call. Which one is your favorite?"

"*The Little Mermaid*," he said, picking the tape up. "I've watched it about a hundred times!"

"Well then, *The Little Mermaid* it is! I really like that one, too."

He turned on the TV/VCR that sat on a folding chair across from the bed and pushed the tape in the slot. Owen plopped himself onto the bed and pushed back so he leaned against the wall.

"I haven't seen this movie in ages," I told him.

"Wanna know why it's my favorite?" he asked.

"Definitely."

"Because Ariel gets to go from the ocean up to the land and be who she's always dreamed of being," he said.

"That's pretty awesome," I said.

We watched the movie in silence until Ursula started singing about poor, unfortunate souls. I looked at Owen and thought how fitting it was. There we sat, two prisoners, watching a VHS copy of The Little Mermaid.

"You know what? We're like Ariel," I said. "We both want to be where we were meant to be. Me, at home with my parents. You, in a place where everyone treats you with love and respect."

"What do you mean? People love me here. Mud loves me."

I feared Owen might get upset, but he looked more confused than anything.

"Mud didn't sound very loving this morning," I said.

"Oh, well, he was just mad because you told him you wanted to leave, and then I said maybe you could. He didn't mean to be unkind," he explained. Again, he defended his brother, regardless of his cruelty. I didn't know if it was Owen's mental challenges or the debt he owed to his brother for saving his life, but he was unable to see how awful Mud truly was to him.

"What if you let me go anyway?" I posed.

Owen's face turned serious. "Mud would be very, very angry with me. Besides, I don't want you to go. I ... I like having you here."

"What if ... what if you came with me? The place where I live is a place where you can be who you've always dreamed of being," I said. "You could bring your Hot Wheels and no one would take them from you."

In the 60 days I'd been there, and in all the time that Owen and I had spent together, I'd never seen that expression on his face. He was elated. His eyes were wide and his smile split his face. The hope I wrote off as dead revived and I waited anxiously for Owen to take me up on my offer.

"That's the nicest thing anyone's ever said to me," he said, the smile still plastered across his face. Then the smile dimmed a little. "But I gotta stay here with Mud."

"Maybe you could just let me go then?" I offered.

"But if you left, who would be my friend?" Owen turned his attention back to Ariel, who was dressed haphazardly in the remnants of a sail and trying to look normal. He laughed at Scuttle's delusional fashion sense, and I sat back and let my hope die once again.

Day 277

A tap at the driver's side window of my truck startled me from my uncomfortable slumber. After my exploration of the little town of Jubilee the previous afternoon, I'd pulled around to the side of Toad in the Hole and settled in for the night. Sure I'd be up before the sun, I was surprised to have to adjust my eyes to the brightness of day.

I twisted around and saw Ruth's face framed perfectly inside the window. I turned the key in the ignition to engage the battery.

"Oh, hey," I said as rolled the window down.

"Rise and shine, sunshine girl!" she said cheerily. "You on a stake out or do you not have anywhere to stay on your little adventure?"

I wiped the sleepy from my eyes and yawned. "I don't have anywhere to stay."

"Someone didn't plan very well." She smirked.

"Well, I was a little delusional and thought I might find him yesterday."

"Ah, to be young and stupid. Come on in and get somethin' to eat." Ruth turned and waved me to come with her. I grabbed my backpack and followed her in.

"Got a bathroom I can use?" I asked. Ruth pointed to the back hall.

I checked myself in the mirror and let out an audible gasp. I looked rough. My hair was matted to one side of my head, and I had a line down the side of my face from where I pressed it into the stitching of the leather. Sleeping in my car did not agree with me. I brushed my teeth and splashed some water on my face. Feeling a little fresher, I went back out into the restaurant.

I took a seat at the counter again while Ruth moved around setting up various things on the workstation on the other side.

"You're opening kind of late, aren't you?" The clock on the wall read 9:04 am.

"Nah," she said. "Factory guys start at 7:00. They barely get up and out the door in time to be there then. No way they're gonna get up earlier just so they can pop in here for breakfast. Rest of the town doesn't open until 10:00."

I know at least one who's willing to get up extra early.

"Makes sense," I said. "I took a drive last night and noticed everything seems to shut down kinda early around here, too."

"Just during the week. Factory families are early risers, which means they're early to bed. You must be one of those big city girls," Ruth said.

"Not at all." I took in the décor of Toad in the Hole a little more than the day before. It was quaint. Wood tables and pictures of John Wayne and horses on the walls gave it a western theme. "This place actually reminds me of a diner back home."

"I'd ask where that is, but I have a feeling you won't tell me." Ruth didn't look up from her task.

"You'd be right," I chuckled. "Thanks for understanding."

"We all have our secrets." She turned around. "But can I ask you a, uh, *generic* question?" I nodded cautiously. "You're not here to tell this guy he's won the lottery, are you?"

"What makes you think that?" I asked as if I didn't already know.

"No one as secretive as you comes bearing good news," she said with one raised eyebrow.

"Quite the opposite of the lottery."

"I didn't think so. Lemme give you some unsolicited advice: think long and hard before you go through with whatever it is. Once you go there, you can't go back."

I folded my arms and leaned on the counter. "You sound like you have some experience in that."

"Darlin', you don't get to be my age and not. I've got more experience in things I wish I could take back than I care to remember." She took a deep breath and let out the memories I stirred up. "If you're gonna hang your ass out here you might as well make yourself useful. Why don't roll up some silverware for me?"

Ruth pulled a big divided bin out from under the counter and set it before me. Then she put a stack of oversized napkins to my right.

"Ever fold up a burrito?" she asked. I nodded. "Good, then you've got this!"

The loud banging of pots and pans came from the kitchen, startling us both.

"Who's back there? All day yesterday you put orders in there and then food magically appeared! I never heard or saw anyone at all!"

"Ha! That's Merle for ya! He much prefers to be a ghost!" Ruth laughed.

I spent the morning helping Ruth prepare for the rest of the day. A few people came in for breakfast: a man who worked at the bank, a mother and daughter in town to pick up some groceries, and an elderly couple making their weekly trip to Toad in the Hole.

By the time lunch rolled around, the knots in my stomach had taken over. I was happy for Ruth to keep me busy filling ketchup and mustard bottles, wiping tables and clearing plates from the few customers she had. But once the clock read 11:55 am, I was forced to face the choice I had made in seeking out my vengeance. What was I going to do when I saw Mud? Moreover, what would he do when he saw me?

The men from the factory started coming in and I did the only thing I could think of: I hid.

"You okay?" I heard a man's voice say. I turned to see an old, balding man wearing a white apron standing behind me.

"Uh ... you must be Merle," I said.

"That's me. You okay?" he reiterated.

"I haven't decided yet," I answered. I peeked out of the doorway nervously.

"You'll get a better view from the kitchen, and no one's gonna see you there," he offered with a nod to his left.

"Thanks." Slightly relieved, I followed Merle to the kitchen and stood where he told me I'd get the best view of the dining room. I watched as, one after another, men dressed in tough work pants, grungy long-sleeved shirts, and work boots filed in. Some of them had hats, which made seeing their faces difficult. But Officer Moore wasn't kidding when she said they all looked alike. I wish Mud had some kind of distinguishing marks that would set him apart from all the others. But I knew in my heart I'd know him when I saw him.

Be brave. Even when you're scared, be brave.

Eventually, all the workers who lunched at Toad in the Hole had arrived and were seated, and Ruth had taken all of their orders. Since she offered just one five-dollar special, Merle got to work on plating up that day's: meatloaf, mashed potatoes, and green beans.

By the time each of the men had gotten their order, my heart sank. He wasn't there. The men who wore hats had turned them around to eat, so I was certain of it.

Feeling safe in Mud's absence from lunch, I helped Ruth clear tables as the men finished, while she took care of their checks.

"Who is this doll you've got workin' for you, Ruth?" one man called out. He tried to pinch my butt, but I grabbed his wrist before he could reach me.

"I'd be careful if I were you. She threatened to shoot a guy's balls off yesterday for talking to me. I'm guessing she'd go for the whole package if you put your hands on me." I released his wrist and watched as his buddies laughed.

The guys around here are all super charming, I thought.

I set a handful of plates in the bussing bin behind the counter. When I turned around, I was greeted by a guy decades younger than the rest of the men.

"Sorry about Sal," the guy said. "Would you be surprised to know he's divorced?"

"Shocked." I laughed. The guy smiled at me, and for the first time I thought about what my life could be like once I eliminated Mud. The notion of a future not consumed with what had happened to me was wonderful. I always dreamed of the kind of life Mom and Dad had together. A life full of love and happiness, of joy.

I quickly dismissed my daydreaming. I had to focus on the task at hand.

"I see you met my grandson, Aiden," Ruth said, handing him a Styrofoam cup filled with soda. "Aiden, this is Mary. She's just passin' through, so don't get any ideas."

Aiden blushed and laughed nervously. "Grandma! I'm sorry for her, too," he said to me.

"No worries. I've known her less than 24 hours and trust me, I already get it."

"Well aren't you two peas in a pod with your sassiness! Have a good rest of your day. And stop by on your way home. I told your mom I would send some food home with you tonight. Hope you enjoyed that meatloaf because it's what's for dinner, too!" Ruth gave Aiden a kiss on the cheek and patted his back.

"Thanks, Grandma." Aiden moved toward the herd of men heading for the door and turned around quickly. "Nice meeting you, Mary."

"You too, Aiden."

I helped Ruth wipe tables and reset them for the rest of the afternoon. Business picked up and got busy enough for Ruth to ask if I'd was interested in earning a little cash.

"I used to have a girl helpin' me but she met some guy online and moved to Biloxi." Ruth rolled her eyes.

"Sure. Who couldn't use some extra cash?" I told her.

I didn't know the menu, but that didn't matter. Everyone who came in knew it backward and forward. All I had to do was write down what they wanted and give the ticket to Merle.

Waiting tables didn't suck as bad as I heard it could. It was probably because I was in a small town restaurant and didn't have to do a whole lot, but the people were nice, and it made me think that when it was all over I might try to get a job at a restaurant in Carson.

"Ahhhh," I moaned as I sat down for the first time in two hours. Maybe I *wouldn't* get a job waiting tables. "My feet and back are killing me. How do you do this all day, every day?"

"I've been doin' this so long my body is basically numb from the waist down." Ruth laughed.

A few of the guys from the factory walked in, and I realized it was a little after 6:00. At least the time went by quickly. The bell rang over the door again and Aiden entered. He smiled at me and then called for his grandmother. Ruth appeared from the kitchen with two oversized containers of food she promised to Aiden's mother.

"Thanks, honey. Tell your mom I'll pop by this week, okay?" she said to him.

"Will do, but, I gotta problem," he said. "My car is dead again. Won't turn over at all. I think it's the alternator. Any chance you can give me a ride home?"

"I can't, darlin'. Marcy up and left me last week and I can't leave Mary here by herself."

"I can take him," I offered.

"Are you sure?" Aiden asked.

"Sure. I mean, you've got food. Your mom is expecting it, so you can't exactly wait until Ruth closes up shop, right? I don't mind, really," I told him.

"Thanks, honey! I'm startin' to wonder how I can get you to stick around here!" Ruth said with a smile.

I would stick around, but I'm pretty sure after I kill Mud I'll have to skip town.

"Ha!" I laughed. I looked at Aiden. "Ready?"

Aiden nodded and he followed me to the truck after I grabbed my backpack from the back room. He climbed in and immediately spotted Peter's rifle. My eyes followed and landed on the rifle before looking up and locking onto his.

"A girl can never be too careful." I gave him a small smile and he returned a cautious one.

Aiden directed me onto the main drag of town, back the direction from which I had come, and across Saw Mill Road. We passed a lumber supply company and a mechanic/body shop/salvage yard. It wasn't too much longer until mailboxes appeared one after another along the road. I wondered if one of them belonged to Mud. They were spread apart by a quarter mile, like most houses in rural areas. Everyone had a nice piece of land they could call their own.

"So how long have you worked at the factory?" I asked, making small talk.

"About two years. Started right out of high school," he said.

"Do you like it?"

"It's honest work."

I understood. I'd watched my father be an honest, hard-working man my whole life. Peter, too. It was nice to see someone else being raised the same way.

"What about you? What do you do?" Aiden asked.

That was hard to answer. The truth was that I'd spent the last six months trying to get over the most horrific thing a person can endure, and the last few days plotting my only way out of the dark cloud that followed me.

"I help my dad on our cattle farm," I told him. It had been true at one point in my life. Aiden didn't need to know it wasn't true now.

"And do you like it?" he said, echoing my question.

"It's honest work." I smiled.

I pulled onto the driveway Aiden pointed out and up to the house. It was old, like most houses in farm and factory country, but looked well maintained.

"Well, thanks again for the ride. Don't suppose you can pick me up in the morning." Aiden let out a breathy laugh.

"Uh, no. I understand you have to be at work at 7:00 am. I am *not* showing up here that early!" I laughed.

Aiden got out and thanked me again before he shut the door. I watched him go inside and then made a U-turn on the gravel driveway before I started back down the driveway. I was almost to the end when I saw that Aiden had left the containers of meatloaf in the seat between us.

I let out a sigh and put the car in reverse. When I got back to the house, I backed into the gravel, got out, and grabbed the containers. The house was quiet as I stepped onto the porch. To my right I saw a ramp, like the kind that would be need for someone in a wheelchair, and wondered who in Aiden's home needed it.

I knocked on the screen door and waited for someone to answer. Aiden came into view and a look of relief flooded his face when he saw me.

"Aww! You are a lifesaver!" he said as he opened the door. "Mamma! Mary came back with the meatloaf!" he called to his mother. "C'mon in!"

"Oh, no, that's okay," I said in protest.

"I insist. You've got to meet my mom. She's the best!"

I understood Aiden's sentiment about his mother and couldn't refuse him a second time. So I crossed the threshold with a smile.

I followed Aiden down a long hall and into the kitchen. There, at a modified counter, sat his mother in a wheel chair. She was soft and sweet looking, with light brown hair she had pulled into a ponytail, fair skin, and pale blue eyes. She was almost angelic.

"You must be Mary! I'm Charlene. Mamma called and said you were giving Aiden a ride home. Thank you so much for that! His daddy is on a hunting trip and won't be back until late. He's normally back on

Sunday night, but he decided to take an extra day this time. Although I have no idea why he goes because he never gets anything!" she laughed.

"Oh, it's no problem," I said. "Well, I better get going. It was nice to meet you both."

"Oh, no! Don't go! Stay and at least have a glass of lemonade," Charlene said. "I make the best in Jubilee!"

I wished the woman didn't remind me so much of my mother, but she did. She was sweet and kind and the most hospitable woman I'd met since my mother. It was hard to refuse her when I knew how much it meant to Mom for people to accept her invitations.

"A glass of lemonade would be lovely, thank you." I smiled and Charlene's doubled in size.

"Wonderful! Aiden, get Mary settled into the living room, and when you come back I'll have the lemonade all ready."

I followed Aiden back down the hallway and into the front living room. It was decorated modestly with a floral sofa and love seat, a recliner, and a coffee table. Above the mantel sat family pictures, and on the walls hung framed reproductions forest scenes.

"Here, have a seat," Aiden said. "I'll be right back."

I nodded and moved toward the love seat. I started to sit down but was drawn to the family pictures above the fireplace. I had a deep appreciation for family pictures. I loved the frames that had a picture of someone as a baby and then an adult picture next to it. It was fun to see if they had changed or just grew into their baby face.

One by one, I took in each picture. It seemed Aiden was an only child because there were no pictures of other kids. There was a picture of Aiden's parents kissing at their wedding, and a few of Charlene with Aiden in a park. She was standing in all of them, so she obviously had an accident that left her unable to walk. My heart was full of happiness for Aiden until I reached a frame with a portrait of his entire family. My heart stopped.

There, standing behind his son and his wheel chair-bound wife, was Mud.

Day 75

"I don't want to watch a movie today, Owen," I told him. I was so sick of kids' movies and cartoons that I wanted to scream. It had been almost a month since Owen began testing the waters and laying down his own rules. I thought for sure he would have limited Mud's access to me even more, but he hadn't. Mud still came in every morning, and every morning he seemed to be more aggressive than the one before.

"Why not? We don't have to watch *The Little Mermaid* again. We can watch whatever you want," he said. "Or we could read a book. I've been practicing on my own."

"I'm tired," I said simply.

"Oh. You're not sleepin' good?"

"No, Owen, I'm not sleeping well. You wanna know why? Because every night I close my eyes knowing that the next time I open them your brother is going to be in here raping me!" I raised my voice and it took Owen by surprise. He stood up, flustered.

"I—I—I," he stuttered.

Shit.

"I'm sorry, Owen. I shouldn't have yelled at you," I said. "I just really, *really* want to go home." I begged him with my words and my eyes. And then the tears fell uncontrollably. "Please, Owen. Please! I just want to go home! I miss my Dad and my Mom so much! And my mom, she still needs me!"

Neither my apology nor my crying helped to settle Owen's flustered state. He left the room, locking the door behind him.

Squeak. Tap. Click.

I lay on the bed and let the tears soak my pillow. This was my life now: a real-life blow-up doll for a sadistic rapist, and a playmate to his mentally challenged brother. My morning would begin with Mud finding new ways to brutally rape me, while the rest of my day would be spent watching children's movies and reading chapter books. Every hope and dream I ever had for my life had shriveled up and died.

I didn't hear the *tap, squeak* of the latch before Owen opened the door. My crying had been loud enough to cover the sound.

"You love your mom and dad a lot," he said.

I sat up and wiped my face with my shirt. "Yes. Very, very much."

Owen sat down at the end of the bed. "What's that like?"

"What do you mean?" I asked. "I know your parents were mean to you, but you still loved them in some way, didn't you?"

"Mud said since they didn't love me back, what I felt for them wasn't really love." He twisted his mouth in contemplation. "But I'm not sure about that."

"How does Mud know they didn't really love you?" I asked. I thought it ironic considering I was positive that whatever Mud felt for his brother was truly a perversion of love.

"Mud said when they found out I was slow, they tried to get rid of me. But County Services wouldn't let them since I wasn't no trouble," he told me. "So they got mad they had to keep me and feed me and stuff."

Owen fidgeted with his hands. I couldn't wrap my brain around the immense sadness he exuded.

"I'm so sorry you went through that," I said. "Loving your parents is great because, well, it's a two-way street. Actually, loving anyone is a two-way street. We give a part of our heart to them, and they give a part of their heart to us. You take care of each other. No one has to be the boss all the time. And you never, ever hurt someone you love on purpose. You don't call them names or hit them, or make them do things they don't want to. That's how I know Mud doesn't love me. He says mean things to me, he hits me, and he makes me do things I don't want to do."

Owen nodded slightly. I wondered if anything I said made sense to him.

"This used to be my room," he said.

"Oh?"

"Yes. That's why Mud said to keep you in here, because the latch was already on the door."

Oh my God. This just gets worse and worse.

"Why did they lock you in your room?" I asked. My brows knitted together so tightly that it hurt my eyes.

"For lots of reasons. I didn't eat fast enough. I didn't walk fast enough, or come quick enough when they called," he said.

"Wait. I only saw one other bedroom. If this was your room, where did your parents and Mud sleep?"

Owen paused before he spoke. "They slept in the big house. I'm not allowed at the big house."

"So they all slept in another house and you slept out here? And they still locked you in this one room?" I wanted to vomit. The atrocities Owen had experienced as a child shocked me at first. But after a second thought, it made sense. It didn't matter that Mud had killed their parents to allegedly protect Owen. Mud was cut from the same sadistic cloth. "Owen? Do you ever wonder why Mud waited so long to protect you from your parents? I mean, Mud got to be a grown up when you were three. He could have helped you then." I held my breath and hoped my question wouldn't upset Owen and send him into another flustered tailspin.

"He said there wasn't ever a good time before that day," Owen answered.

Of course he gave Owen a bullshit answer.

"Owen, can't you see that Mud—"

"I don't want to talk about that anymore. It's making me sad." Owen stood and left the room. He returned quickly with a movie in one hand and a book in the other. "*Pete's Dragon* or *Amelia Bedelia?*"

I let out a gust of air, puffy cheeks and all. "Pete's Dragon," I said.

I could use some tips on manifesting an imaginary dragon right about now.

The movie ended and Owen stayed to himself for the rest of the day. He brought me lunch and dinner, but didn't stay or chat. I had stirred up some emotions that were still raw. Considering Mud was Owen's only confidant, I felt sure no one exactly encouraged Owen to deal with the trauma he had experienced. But I also couldn't shake the thought that Owen understood more than he let on. I wondered if he was so used to believing whatever Mud told him that, when his gut instincts kicked in, he pushed them aside because that's what Mud told him to do. I hoped my presence and the pot I had stirred reminded him of those gut feelings, and that I was one step closer to removing the scales from Owen's eyes. Unless he could see Mud clearly, he'd never do anything to fully go against his brother. Moreover, until he saw Mud for who he really was, I'd never be able to get him to leave that place with me.

Day 277

Shit. Shit. Shit. Shit. Shit. Shit. Shit.

Oh my God! Oh my God! Oh my God! Oh my God!

I sprinted to the truck and sped out of there so fast it looked like I was trying to outrun a sandstorm. Not only had I found Mud, but I found his whole fucking family! His mother-in-law had befriended me! And his hospitable wife was in a fucking wheelchair!

I drove in a panic. I needed a plan. My only one had been to find Mud and kill him. Somehow I thought I'd get to town, see him, follow him to his car and shoot him in cold blood. Still a fine plan in my mind, but that was before Aiden and Charlene.

Oh my God. Do they know? Are they one of those creepy couples where as along as hubby is happy, we're all happy?

No, no. Stop, Caroline. That's ridiculous. Think.

He has a family. And all the time he spent at Owen's, they thought he was out hunting. Should I tell her? She'd never believe me. Oh no. *What if he's holding another girl captive, and he told them he was hunting, but he's really there doing the same horrific things to her as he did to me?* Should I go back? Look for Owen's house? It had to be behind their house—the big house—through the woods. Owen told me not to take the path. It must lead to the house.

What do I do? Now that I'm here, what do I do?

I got to the edge of town and pulled over so I could think.

I need to call Officer Moore. I picked up my phone and entered my password, but then stared at the screen with her contact information. My finger hovered above the little telephone next to her name.

Office Moore said all they needed was a new lead. Everything they needed was on a silver platter right there. I could make it so easy for them. Just one call and they'd be here in a matter of hours, and everything would wrap up in a neat little bow.

Calling her would be the smart thing to do.

Calling her would be the responsible thing to do.

No. I'm not calling her. They had their chance to find Mud and bring him to justice. It was my turn. This was *my* journey to find *my* closure. I had come too far to let that go.

My heart calmed and my mind cleared. I knew what I needed to do. I just had to figure out how to do it.

I drove back to Toad in the Hole and parked next to the building. When I went in, Ruth immediately addressed me.

"What happened to you?" she called. "Charlene called and said you had taken out of there like a rat lookin' for cheese!"

"I'm really sorry," I said. "I got a call from a friend with a problem she *couldn't* wait on and I just got side tracked. I was gonna go back, but then I felt bad."

That was the worst excuse ever.

"Well," Ruth gave me her best side eye, "we don't do that sorta thing around here."

"Tell you what? How about I go back tomorrow while the men are at work and keep Charlene company for a bit? Think that would smooth things over?" I kept my tone light and sweet.

"I think that would be very nice of you," Ruth agreed. "Was Hudson back from his hunting trip yet?"

Hudson? His name is Hudson? It made sense. Kids mess up names all the time when they're little. Owen must have tried to say his name but the "H" came out as an "M" and it stuck. And of course, none of his fellow factory workers would know. But ... what about Ruth? Did she know?

"Um, no," I said. "I knew a guy named Hudson once. He went by all sorts of nicknames because he hated it. What about Charlene's husband?"

Wow, Caroline. Be a little more obvious!

"Not as far as I know. He's never asked any of us to call him any different," she said. She moved behind the counter and Merle clanked things around in the kitchen as they prepared for closing.

I wiped the tables down and refilled the shakers and condiment bottles. Then I swept the dining room, all the while working on a plan. Getting into Charlene's house was the first step. It would have to be while Aiden and Mud were at work. Spend a little time with Charlene, and then find Owen's house.

Seven rolled around, and I followed Merle and Ruth out as she locked the door.

"Later, Merle!" Ruth called as my new silent friend walked to his car. He waved and said he'd see her us in the morning.

I started toward my truck. "Thanks for letting me hang out today. I'll see you in the morning."

"Where do you think you're going?" she said in a correcting tone.

"I'm headed to my truck," I said hesitantly.

"No ma'am, you are not. I can't have you sleepin' in your truck. Too many nights of that and you'll be useless to me. Now, I don't know how long you'll stick around, but as long as you're here … well, you were a real lifesaver today. The boys are used to bein' patient with me, but things went a lot smoother with you there. I've got an extra room with a moderately comfortable bed. You'll be stayin' with me as long as you're in Jubilee."

I opened my mouth to refuse her offer, but the look she gave cut me off.

"That's very kind of you, Ruth. Thank you."

Ruth had an apartment above Toad in the Hole, which we accessed through an entrance in the back of the building. We took the long flight of stairs up to a single door at the top and entered. It wasn't what I expected. I thought, considering the age of the building, that I'd find it a little run down, but it was quite the opposite. It looked like one of those upscale lofts you see in magazines. The floors were a high-gloss, dark wood, and the exposed brick was striking. Two thick, square wooden poles divided her living area from the dining. The look on my face must have revealed my surprise.

"It ain't what you thought it was gonna be, is it?" Ruth asked with a smirk.

"Um, no," I said with a breathy laugh. "Sorry!"

Ruth chuckled. "Don't be sorry! I like the 'wow' factor."

"It's definitely 'wow'!" I tossed my backpack on Ruth's leather couch and joined her in the kitchen. I watched her pull some containers from the fridge and bread from the cabinet.

She has no clue what her son-in-law is.

No one in Jubilee knew. It made me wonder if my plan of killing him was enough. Maybe I should haul his ass into the middle of town and expose him for the monster he was. Was death too good for him? It only took a second to answer. No. Death was everything he deserved.

Pictures on the fridge caught my eye. I scanned them and saw more pictures of Aiden than anyone. In some of them he was little and with friends from school. In others he was big, like maybe they were only a few years old. There were only two of him with his father, and four with his mother.

"I'm guessing Aiden is your only grandchild," I said.

"Yep. He's the apple of my eye," she said. "Charlene was an only child and so is Aiden. I guess it was inevitable since she married an only child, too."

Wait. What? Mud wasn't an only child. Holy shit! Rage started to boil in me and my breathing became shallow. My nostrils flared, too. Mud had kept Owen locked away in that house his whole life? *Oh, Owen. If you could only see!*

"You okay?" Ruth asked, seeing the change in my demeanor.

I took a cleansing breath. "Oh, yeah, I'm good," I said. "You ever have a thought that runs through your mind and it just lights a fire in your belly?"

"I know the feeling." She laughed as she assembled sandwiches. "You don't get to live this long and not have memories that haunt you. I hope you like chicken salad."

"Love it!" I told her. The fact that I was keeping it together deserved an Oscar. All I wanted to do was hop in my truck and go back to Aiden's house and kill his son of a bitch father. But I couldn't rush it. If I was going to do it, I couldn't run in, guns blazing. I had to be systematic about it.

She poured two glasses of lemonade, and we took our meal out to the dining table.

Time for a little fact gathering.

"How long have you lived in Jubilee?" I asked.

"I moved here when Charlene was a baby," she answered.

I took a bite of my sandwich. "This is *really* good, Ruth! Why isn't it on the menu downstairs?"

"I gotta keep some things for myself. If I put everything on the menu, I'd never eat at home. If I don't eat at home, I'd never have any down time," she explained.

"That makes so much sense," I replied. "So it was just you, Charlene's father, and Charlene when you moved?"

"Nope, just me and Charlene. Me and her daddy had a fallin' out when she was an infant. He'd slap me around and was generally pretty evil, so we left. He tried to weasel his way back into our lives over the years, but I stood my ground and he eventually gave up. He'd bring flowers and gifts and throw on the same charm he used to get me to fall in love with him. But he never stayed for long and it got real confusing for Charlene, especially when she was around eight or nine. I used to worry she'd end up with someone like him, but she got a real good one in Hudson."

I had taken a sip of lemonade and choked on it when she delivered that last line.

"You okay?" Ruth leaned over and patted my back. "Raise your arms over your head!"

I did as she instructed and worked hard to swallow the load of shit she was dishing out. It wasn't her fault. All Mud had given them had been a heaping pile of it, so that's all she had to serve.

"Yeah, yeah, I'm good. It just went down the wrong way," I said as I caught my breath. "Sounds like this Hudson guy is one of a kind. How'd Charlene meet him?"

"They were high school sweethearts." Ruth beamed with joy, recalling those sweet memories. "Inseparable. Joined at the hip!" she laughed. "It took me an hour to get him out of the house at the end of the night! They had a beautiful little wedding and Aiden came along right away. He's a chip off the old block. Just like his daddy." *I hope not.* "After Charlene's accident, Aiden was right there next to his daddy taking care of her. Napkin?"

"Yes. Thank you. What happened?"

The joy on Ruth's face dropped and was replaced by sorrow. "Oh, it was just tragic! Hudson had been out on a hunting trip and Aiden was at school. So, Charlene being Charlene, she went outside to tend to wild bushes at the tree line behind the house. Well, she swore she heard someone crying and moved deeper into the woods to see if she could find whoever it was." *Owen? Another girl?* "That's when she tripped, twisted, and slammed her back on a rock. Doctors said she was lucky. Another inch and she would've been paralyzed from the neck down. Thank God Hudson came back early; otherwise she would have laid out there for hours."

The list of things Mud had destroyed was growing, and so was my concern for what I might find in the little house in the woods. I couldn't be sure that the crying Charlene heard was Owen. It could have been another girl. If it was, how many were there between her and me? Had Owen let them escape? If not, where were they now?

Day 80

Eighty days. That's how long it takes to realize you're in a psychotically comfortable pattern as a prisoner, sex slave, and babysitter. And, after that morning's episode, I wondered if Mud was getting comfortable, too. His aggression had retreated to the level it had been when he was able to visit me twice a day. It was rough, and it never stopped being traumatic, but I didn't wonder if he was going to actually kill me, so there was that.

After the usual routine, Mud finally left and Owen returned with my breakfast. He'd been making me omelets since I raved about that first one. I scarfed it down and Owen returned empty-handed.

"Have we run out of movie and book options?" I asked.

Owen looked down, seeming a little shy to ask me what was on his mind. "Um ... I was wonderin' if we could play a game?"

"Oh, sure. That'd be a nice change of pace," I told him with a smile. He reciprocated with a beaming smile of his own and darted from the room. I heard him rummaging through a closet or bin of games. The sound of game pieces like tokens and checkers clattered together as they slid from one side of their box to the other. The commotion finally ended and Owen returned with a game that looked like a tiny suitcase.

"Is that backgammon?" I asked. Owen nodded cautiously. "I LOVE backgammon!"

"Really?" Owen's excitement was palpable. I liked seeing him so happy, but scolded myself internally for having shown so much excitement of my own. It only encouraged Owen and reinforced his rationalization to keep me there as his playmate.

Owen opened the game board flat on the bed and began to set up the pieces.

"Mud doesn't like to play games with me," he said. "He says I take too long, especially with backgammon cuz I have to do math."

"That's not very nice of Mud," I pointed out. "Are there any games he *does* like to play with you?"

"No. We just watch movies."

"Sex movies?" Owen nodded his answer without making eye contact with me. "What about other kinds of movies, like super heroes?" Again, Owen nodded silently while he set up the game.

Even if Mud never laid a hand on me, I would hate him for what he had done to Owen. He may have saved his life, but Owen might have been better off dead than living in that prison.

Owen rolled the dice and, after taking a minute to count, moved his first pieces along the board to their resting place.

"Good job," I told him. I took my turn and moved my pieces as well, much more quickly than he had.

"You're fast," Owen observed.

"I've just had more practice. If Mud would play with you, you'd get more practice, too," I told him.

Owen rolled and then looked up at me. "But now I have you, and you can help me practice." I gave him a tense smile and a single nod.

We played two games by lunchtime. Owen begged to play one more round before we ate, but I was getting pretty hungry and each game had taken us over an hour to play. So we packed the board and pieces up and clicked the case closed. When Owen came back, he had two plates in his hands.

"Is it okay if I eat lunch with you?" he asked sweetly. My heart broke for the man's loneliness.

"Of course."

Owen set our food down on the bed and retrieved our drinks. As he sat down, I knew it was a good time to plant some more seeds of doubt about his brother.

"Where does Mud go all day?" I asked. I focused my eyes on my sandwich to be as nonchalant as possible.

Owen took a bite of his sandwich and answered with a mouth full of peanut butter and jelly. "He works at the factory."

"Oh yeah? What does he do there?"

"I don't know."

"Oh." I paused and drank some milk before continuing. "How come you don't work at the factory, too? I bet you'd be a really good worker there."

"Mud says I'm not smart enough to work at the factory. There's too much dangerous equipment. He says I might mess it up," he answered matter-of-factly.

I contained my rage before I replied. "I don't think that's true at all! I think you're very smart!"

"Really?" Owen looked like he'd never heard anyone tell him he was smart before. And he hadn't.

"Yes! And I don't understand why Mud would say you aren't smart. It's like he doesn't even know you." I pulled a piece of my sandwich off and tucked it into my mouth. "I mean, I've known you for 80 days and I even I know how smart you are."

Owen's brows pulled together curiously. I could see the wheels in his head begin to turn. They were turning slowly, but that was okay. They just needed to turn.

Day 278

I woke with a fire in my belly and the smell of bacon wafting into my nose.

Bacon and revenge. What a wonderful way to start the day.

I brushed my teeth, got dressed, and pulled my hair up into a ponytail. Then I put my ball cap on and met Ruth in the kitchen.

"Okay. That might be the most comfortable bed ever," I said as I entered the kitchen. "Thanks for not letting me sleep in the truck again."

"Purely selfish on my part, but I'm glad you reaped some benefits as well!" She laughed. I laughed with her and poured a cup of coffee into the empty mug in front of the coffee maker. "There's cream in the fridge and sugar on the table."

"Perfect!" I poured some cream in my mug and moved to the table to complete the sweetening process. I took a small sip and put the mug down to let it cool, then joined Ruth. "What can I do to help?"

She took two plates down from the cabinet and placed them next to the stove where she had been moving scrambled eggs around. Then she opened the microwave and revealed a plate of bacon she'd already made and put in there to keep warm.

"Not a thing." Ruth served up the plates and took a pan of biscuits out of the oven.

"Oh wow! Those smell amazing."

"Breakfast ain't breakfast without biscuits," she said.

"Agreed!"

I sat at the table drinking coffee and eating a delicious breakfast made by the mother-in-law of the man I was going to kill. She was so sweet and kind, I almost hated to hurt her that way, but the truth of who Mud was would have to come to light. Once they all knew what a monster he was, they would understand.

"So, did Hudson make it back last night?" I asked. I hated calling him that. I didn't care that it was his real name. His nickname was much more fitting.

"Yeah. Charlene texted me last night we he got in. Also to let me know that she'd love to have you come by today. I texted her earlier and told her you wanted to," Ruth said.

"Oh, great. I'm glad you did that. I'd hate to surprise her again," I said. "I'll help you get things set up downstairs and then go over. I'll try to be back to help with the lunch rush."

Ruth stood and took her plate to the kitchen. I ate my last piece of bacon and followed suit.

"No need to rush. Those men have been doin' fine with just me waitin' on them. They can handle another day. I'd rather Charlene have some company out there for a bit. I think it'll do her some good." Ruth smiled and put her hand on my shoulder. "I don't know what you've got planned, Mary, but I sure do hope you'll consider stickin' around here."

I gave her a thin smile. "That's very kind of you."

It only took about an hour to get Toad in the Hole set up for the day since we had done so much the night before. Ruth packed up some leftover pies she decided not to sell, so I'd have a little peace offering when I showed up at Charlene's.

"Make sure you tell her you've got some key lime pie in there. That's her favorite!"

I promised I would and pushed the door open, letting a warm gust of air wash over my body. I put the pies in the car and checked to make sure my rifle, gun, and cap bolt gun were exactly where I left them. Fortunately, in small, sleepy towns, no one bothers with other people's things. Too few suspects.

My heart pounded inside my chest the closer I got to Mud's house. The big house. The place he lived a lie and deceived people who loved him. It made me sick that Charlene and Aiden lived under the same roof as that sadistic man. When all was said and done, and they knew the monster he was, they would thank me.

I painted on a smile and pulled the truck up as close to the side of the house as I could without it looking odd. If I got the chance I was hoping for to snoop around the house, I would need the truck close if I had to make a quick escape.

With pies in hand, I rapped on the screen door and waited for Charlene to appear. I heard the wheels of her chair on the wood floors before her sweet face appeared around the corner from a back room.

"Mary, I'm so glad you came!" Charlene's joyful voice contributed to my already breaking heart. "Please come in." She leaned toward the door and pushed it toward me. I took it in my free hand and pulled it the rest of the way open, stepping inside.

"Well, I just wanted to apologize for taking off so suddenly yesterday. I let a girlfriend of mine suck me into her drama and, well … I'm here now. Oh! And I brought pies!" I extended the stack of pies in my hands with a huge smile on my face.

"My mother is so funny. I bet she sent some key lime, didn't she?"

"I was told *specifically* to make sure you knew it was in here." I laughed.

"She knows me so well! Let's get those in the fridge." Charlene motioned her hand to follow her. She rolled herself into the kitchen and opened the fridge. "Do you mind putting them on that top shelf? If they're up there I'll be forced to wait for Aiden and Hudson to get home before I indulge."

"Smart move." I did as she asked and closed the fridge. Charlene asked if she could get me anything, but I was still satisfied from breakfast with Ruth, so I followed her out to the screened in porch in the back of the house. The house was old, but the porch looked like it had recently received some love. The white paint was fresh and crisp and the furniture looked new.

"This is lovely," I said as I sat in a wicker love seat. The cushion was a pretty red and blue paisley.

"Thank you! When the weather got nicer, I held Hudson to his promise of fixing up the porch. We were going to do it last year, but his job got so demanding. He was going in early and staying late. They even had him going in on some weekends." *Liar.* "And when he wasn't at the factory he was hunting. With as hard as he was working, I just couldn't take that away from him. So his Honey-Do list got pushed back and pretty long!"

I bit my tongue long enough to let the rage in me subside. "Well, he did a great job." I looked out to the woods, straining my eyes to see if I could find Owen's hidden prison. "How far back does your property go?"

"We have about 10 acres, but most of it is woods. One day we'll get back there and do something with it. This was Hudson's parents' house, and they weren't much for doing anything with the land," she told me.

"Oh," I said. "So did you all live here together?"

"Oh, no. Hudson and I lived in a tiny little house way on the other side of town when we first got married. But then his parents had a tragic accident, and we moved in after that."

"I'm so sorry to hear that. How did they die?" I asked. I wondered what load of bullshit story Mud had given to his beloved.

"Well, it really was a freak accident. Harold was going to clean his gun and apparently Clara was standing right behind him when it went off. It was so awful. It blew right through his head and into hers!" Charlene covered her heart with her hand. "Poor Hudson found them."

What a load of crock! Who in their right mind would believe that story? He obviously had the whole town deceived. The police didn't see through that crap?

"That is very tragic," I agreed.

"What about you, Mary? Are your parents still with us?" she asked.

"No. Both my parents passed a while ago. And I don't have any siblings, so it's just me." It was only a half lie.

"Mama said you were in town looking for someone. Have you found them yet?"

"Not yet. But I think I'm close."

"If there's anything we can do to help, just let me know. Hudson knows everyone in Jubilee, so he'd be a good resource for you, if you'd like," she offered.

"Well, maybe I'll corner him and shake all the information I can out of him." I smiled and gave a small laugh. Poor Charlene laughed too. She had no idea the storm that was about to blow through and demolish their lives. I didn't relish the idea of destroying this poor, sweet woman and her son's lives, but my resolve to annihilate Mud trumped everything else.

"It's beautiful, isn't it?" Charlene asked. I was staring out into the woods, and she mistook my glare for awe. While she looked at the trees and saw the wonder of their creation, I saw through them to the evil that lurked.

I wondered what Owen was doing. Was he playing with his Hot Wheels or watching a cooking show? Was there a girl trapped in the bedroom like I had been? Had she bonded with Owen as well? It took everything in me not to dart out the back door and down the narrow path. I didn't know how far back the little house would be, but I knew it was there, and I knew Owen was inside.

"Oh, yes. It's mesmerizing," I said. "Hudson's parents never did anything with the property through the woods?"

"Well, not really. There's an old shack out there that Hudson calls his man cave. He keeps his tools and those awful guns out there. He's not allowed to keep weapons in the house," she said. "I know they're for hunting, but I just can't stomach having them nearby."

"Well, that makes sense." *And gives me some useful information.* I'd be surprised if there really were any guns in Owen's house. "My dad used to have a gun in the house and my mother hated it as well. 'Guns are for taking down animals and should be used accordingly', she would say."

Charlene chuckled. "I agree 100 percent!"

"Do you mind if I ask about your accident?" I twisted my mouth nervously, unsure if she'd be willing to talk about that terrible day.

"Of course," she answered with a smile.

"Ruth said you thought you heard someone crying in the woods. Did that happen a lot?"

Charlene pursed her lips, seemingly unsure of how to answer. "Actually … yes. But when I told Hudson, you'd have thought I said I saw an alien. He said it was preposterous when I was just concerned that someone had gotten lost and may be hurt. Those are thick woods out there," she said.

"Did it sound like a man or a woman?" I asked.

"The day of the accident was the third time I'd heard it. The first two were pretty faint, but that was because I was closer to the house working in the garden. I couldn't be sure, but it may have been a woman. But the third time? I was right up at the edge of the woods and heard it much clearer. I'm certain it was."

"What did your neighbors say? Did they ever hear anything?"

"No one's lived in that house for over 10 years," she said, pointing back toward town. "And the neighbors on the other side have twice as much land and built their house at the far end, so they wouldn't have heard a thing."

He had the perfect scenario. No one around for miles except two people who thought he walked on water.

"What about time the time frame in between then and now?" The expression on Charlene's face told me I was getting curiously nosey, so I thought of a reasonable lie I could tell her. "I'm sorry. There's a story out of Clary about a group of girls who went missing a few years back on a hike. They never turned up, so I guess my interest was piqued."

"Oh, well ... the times I heard crying were a few months apart, so I don't think it'd be those girls. But that's so sad." Charlene frowned and I wanted to tell her that she didn't know a fraction of the horrors that happened out in those woods.

I spent the afternoon getting to know the woman who had no clue who her husband really was. She spoke of him being loving and generous, and how, if she were lucky, Aiden would grow up to be just like his father. We ate lunch and had pie, and talked about the garden she used to have before her accident. And Charlene asked about my family and upbringing, for which I gave her vague and mostly bogus answers.

Before I knew it, three hours had passed. I still had some snooping to do on the property. If I weren't careful, I'd still be there when Mud got home, so I had to make my exit before I ran out of time.

"Well, Charlene, this has been really nice. Thank you for letting me come by today. And, again, I'm sorry for taking off so quickly yesterday," I said as I stood.

"Are you sure you have to go? Hudson and Aiden will be home in," she checked her watch, "oh, well I guess it'll be a couple of hours. But I know Hudson would love to meet you," she said.

I'm sure I'm the last person Hudson *wants to see. Besides, when I see your dirt bag of a husband, I'll be at the trigger end of a .22-caliber rifle.*

"Yeah, I really need to go. I've got some things to do before I get back to the restaurant to help Ruth. But I'm sure I'll be back. I definitely want to meet this Hudson of yours." My cheeks hurt from the fake smile I plastered across my face.

I opened the front door and pushed the screen door open. Charlene rolled into place right behind me.

"Thanks again for a lovely time. Tell Aiden I said hello."

I got into my truck and waved at Charlene before I backed up and turned so I could drive straight down the path to the road. Once on the other side of the trees that hid the house from view, I turned down the driveway of the abandoned house next door. I backed the truck in between the trees and the house to keep it as inconspicuous as possible. Before I got out, I grabbed my father's gun. I didn't plan on using it, but I felt better having it near me if I was going exploring.

Ducking under branches and pushing shrubs aside, I shoved my way into the woods. I was a good quarter mile from Charlene's door and could only guess how far I might need to go before I found the narrow path that led from the back of their house to Mud's so-called "man cave." I tried to move in as straight a line as I could to ensure I didn't cross over to the path before I would be hidden from Charlene's view. She loved that back porch and chances were good she went right back out there after I left.

I had walked for about 10 minutes when decided to veer my course. I moved slow and steady, unlike the last time my feet touched the floor of those woods. When I escaped, I ran as fast as I could until I was sure Owen's house was so far in the distance that I wouldn't be able to see it if I had turned around. I never turned around, though, so…

My heart stopped, causing my feet to do the same. I was still a ways off, but the little house that had been my prison for 99 days came into view through the trees. I swallowed hard and forced myself not to cry. I pushed forward for a better look, asking myself again, now that I was there, what was I going to do? I didn't have time to answer because a dark green truck rolled down the path and stopped in front of the little house. Mud was home early. Before I had time to draw a breath, he stepped out and closed the truck door with a loud bang. I don't know if he sensed he was being watched, but he scanned the woods in my direction before opening the door to the house and going in.

I drew my gun just like Dad taught me and took another five steps toward the house when I stopped. It wasn't the right time. It would be so easy to walk in and shoot Mud right there in Owen's living room. He wouldn't see me coming and would be dead before I had chance to make sure the last thing he heard was my voice telling him that he was about to get exactly what he deserved.

No. I wanted to make Mud sweat. I wanted him to know I was there and that I wasn't afraid of him. By the time I was done with him, I wanted him more afraid of me than he had been of anything in his life.

Day 85

I watched the leaves fall from the trees while I waited for Mud to arrive. The sun rose through the woods and lit their gorgeous shades of yellow and orange. They had changed color over the last couple of weeks and had begun to die, the wind blowing through and snipping them from their branches. I knew the air was chilly. It was my favorite time of year. Dad and I would rake the leaves under the big tree by the house and then jump in the pile. We didn't even care that it meant we had to rake them all up again. I wondered if Dad was raking leaves and thinking the same thing.

Squeak. Tap.

I sat up at the signal that Mud was there for his morning fun. He opened the door looking as much like a monster as he did every other time. I had been smart with him the other day. When he told me to tell him how big his penis was, I replied with, "Oh, is that what that is?" My left side was still sore from his right hook. So I kept my mouth shut and waited for his abrupt instructions.

"Stand up," he barked.

I did as he said.

"Take your pants off."

I unbuttoned my jeans and pushed them down my legs, pulling them off, and shoving them to the side. I wasn't wearing any panties. The ones Owen had gotten me had disappeared when he took them to wash, and the ones I was wearing the day Mud took me got ripped in two.

"Lay on your back."

This was the most time he'd ever taken with me. He usually came in, told me to strip, and then either pushed me onto the bed or turned me around and bent me over.

He undid his pants and dropped them to his knees, then lifted my legs straight up in the air. He held them at the ankles and entered me … slowly. I felt my face scrunch together in confusion. It was sad that the act of Mud's penis in my vagina wasn't what was disturbing anymore, but the fact that he had changed things up.

Something wasn't working right. Mud wasn't enjoying this episode and started to move my legs around. It was weird and awkward, and after a few minutes he gave up. He pulled his pants up and left me.

Squeak. Tap. Click.

Maybe he was losing his—*whatever*—for me. If so, that could mean one of two things: he'd let me leave, or he would kill me. Once he had no use for me, those would be his only options, and somehow I didn't think he was going to give me a ride back to Anderson's.

Time was of the essence. I had to get Owen to let me go. It was proving to be a tough sell, considering Owen saw me as his friend and playmate. I could flip things on him and reject him. Then he wouldn't want me around. But I couldn't do that to him. Mud's mind games were already enough. I couldn't bring myself to be someone else in his life that hurt him.

The only way Owen was going to see Mud for who he really was would be if Mud discovered the truth of what Owen and I did all day, or rather, weren't doing. Mud went to work every morning thinking Owen picked up where he left off. He acquiesced to Owen's once-a-day directive, but wasn't happy about it. If he found out that Owen hasn't laid a finger on me, he'd flip his lid.

Of course, a plan like that could backfire entirely on me. But what's the worst that could happen? He'd keep me locked up as his sex slave or he'd kill me. If the former were his choice, I'd work to make the latter a reality. I had nothing to lose. I could only hope that the ramifications to Owen weren't too serious. Desperate times called for desperate measures, though.

Tap. Squeak.

The door opened and Mud appeared again. This time he looked as he normally did: evil. He slammed the door shut and charged at me.

"Take your fucking pants off," he demanded.

I slid them off faster than I ever had before. His tame attempt had thrown me for a loop, and once he was back with renewed aggression, my emotions were tossed around even more. My heart pounded, and raging electrical currents raced along my nerves. I hadn't felt like that in weeks.

Once my pants lay in crumpled pile on the floor, Mud turned me around and bent me over the bed. I rested the weight of my body on my forearms while my neck relaxed my head onto the bed. Without warning, as he always did, Mud grabbed my hips and slammed into me, letting out a gurgling groan that made me want to vomit. He didn't give me any instructions to say or do anything. Instead he said something through gritted teeth.

"Told him that gentle shit wasn't for me."

A few more thrusts and Mud let out his signature moan as he pulled out and came on my back. I had become accustomed to a lot of things in my time there, but the feeling of his disgusting fluid on my body would never be one of them.

I lifted my arm back so he could release the handcuff. As soon as he did, he was gone, and I was turning the shower on and opening the box to the new bar of Dove soap. In 85 days I had only used bar soap to wash my body and my hair. I couldn't complain. At least I got to bathe.

I lathered the soap and rubbed my hands across every inch of my body, hoping and praying as I did every day that I wasn't pregnant.

I finished quickly as I always did and dressed in time to see Mud open the door. I stood next to the bed and held out my arm. He attached the handcuff and left. The old Mud was back, having kicked the ass of the new Mud who had made a short-lived appearance.

After Mud was gone, I used the comb Owen had given me and ran it through my hair. Owen arrived with my breakfast and immediately wanted to play backgammon. We must have played twenty times in the last few days. He was legitimately getting better to the point where I wasn't throwing games to boost his ego like I used to do with my little cousins.

"Oh my gosh! I can't believe you beat me again, Owen." I smiled as we set the board up again.

"Aww ... you're lettin' me win." he blushed.

"No, I'm not! I swear." I held up my left hand and put my right one over my heart. Owen gave me a knowing look and I caved. "Okay, okay! I did a few times at first, but you are seriously getting good. Your strategy is awesome."

Owen blushed and moved our black and white discs back to their places on the board. I turned to watch the leaves again while I waited. I longed to be outside, even if just for a minute. Owen stuck to Mud's instructions to leave me locked up while he was gone, so I was positive he wouldn't consider letting me breathe some air that wasn't filled with the stench of my rape.

"You like the leaves?" Owen asked.

I turned and looked at him with soft eyes. "Yes. My dad and I used to jump in them after we raked them up. I miss that. I miss him." I lowered my eyes.

"I bet that's fun," he said. "It sounds like something I'd like to do. But I don't think Mud would let me."

"Why not?"

"I gotta be real quiet when I go outside. Mud says we don't want the neighbors to get upset with us for being too loud," he explained.

One hundred points to me for not rolling my eyes. I was so sick of how Mud treated Owen.

"Owen?" I began. I picked up the dice and rolled them between my hands. "Mud was different this morning. Do you know why he was so different?" I wondered if Owen could clarify what Mud meant when he said "that gentle shit" wasn't for him.

"Oh, well, I told Mud I didn't want him to be so rough with you anymore. I thought you'd like that," he explained.

"I would have preferred that, except ... he wasn't gentle. He was very rough like he normally is," I told him.

"What?" Owen looked genuinely surprised. "But he said—"

"He lied to you, Owen."

Owen looked down. Sadness washed over his face and his eyes darted from side to side as he tried to make sense of what I had just said. Then he looked up and straight into my eyes.

"Or maybe *you're* lying to me."

"What? No! Why would I lie to you?" I protested.

"Because you want to go home and I want you to stay here with me," he said. He began taking the pieces off the backgammon board and putting the game away.

"Yes, I want to go home, but I've always said that. Owen, please believe me. I would never lie to you." I took hold of Owen's wrist to get him to stop cleaning up the game and to look at me. "Owen!" He finally stopped and lifted his head so he could see me. "Just ask him. While he was ... here ... he said, 'I told him that gentle stuff wasn't for me.' Why don't you just ask him?"

Owen didn't say anything else. He closed the game board, slid it under the bed, and left.

Squeak. Tap. Click.

It was hours before I heard any commotion outside my door. Mud slammed the door to the house when he arrived, so I always knew when he was there. I was surprised he still came over, considering he wasn't allowed to touch me in the evening. Yet, there he was. I listened for more to happen than the mumblings of their mundane conversation or Mud's whining that he didn't get a go at me after work.

It was quiet for a while, until I was certain Owen wasn't going to say anything. I hated stirring that pot, but if Owen was ever going to see his brother's true colors, I had to turn up the heat and get out my spoon. If Owen told Mud he knew what he said to me while he was in here, then Mud would know we carried on a conversation. I had a feeling that wasn't going to go over too well.

The mumbling of their conversation got louder, and before I knew it, I heard the quickest *tap, squeak* since I'd been there.

The door flew open and Mud stood there narrowing his eyes at me.

"You don't talk to my brother!" he yelled. "Unless he tells you to, you stay quiet as a fucking mouse! Do you hear me?" I nodded. Owen was standing behind him with trepidation oozing from his eyes. "He's dumb as a stump, so he don't need you confusin' him. He comes in, he fucks you, and he leaves. Got it?"

I nodded again.

"Got it?" he reiterated.

"Got it."

Day 279

An almost eerie calm had washed over me since I saw Mud through the woods. Perhaps because I was in control. I had the upper hand, and he had no idea I was there. He had successfully avoided the police during their investigation and had been living comfortably in his community for nine months. Meanwhile, I'd had been existing in the nightmare he created for me. Well, the tables were about to turn.

I helped Ruth set up Toad in the Hole as I had for the past few days. I felt like a regular employee there. I was learning the ropes on the floor and even helping Merle in the kitchen. If I wasn't about to murder one of their residents, I might actually be able to be happy in Jubilee.

"Charlene said she had a real nice time with you yesterday," Ruth said. She brought out a large bin with napkins and silverware for me to roll.

"She is so sweet," I said. "I wish I had stayed longer, but I felt like I was wearing out my welcome." I chuckled and pulled a stack of napkins from the bin.

"I'm glad to hear you say that, because she's invited us for dinner tonight after we close up."

"Is she sure it won't be too late?" I asked.

"I close up at 4:00 on Fridays," she said.

"Really?"

"Oh, yeah. Toad in the Hole ain't exactly a hot date location," she laughed. "Folks drive into Anesbury or Chapel on Friday and Saturday nights." Ruth looked absolutely thrilled, but the expression on my face told her I wasn't sure. "Aiden will be there," she said in a singsong tone.

"Oh, I see what's going on here." I laughed. "This is all about setting me up with your grandson!"

"What? He's a good boy. You're a good girl. I don't see anything wrong with two good people spending some time together." Ruth's eyebrows went halfway up her forehead like her matchmaking was no big deal. If they only knew.

Aiden was a nice guy, and in another reality I might be up for a little matchmaking. But in the world I lived in, that was impossible.

But...

The wheels in my head started turning at a furious speed. What better way to let Mud know I was there and in control than through his son? The idea of playing a little mind game with him intrigued me. I'd hold all the cards and he'd have nothing, be able to do nothing.

"Oh, all right! Twist my arm why don't you!" I laughed. "Dinner with Charlene's family sounds wonderful."

"Ha! I knew you had your eye on him!" Ruth sounded off in victory. The door opened and the bell signaled the end of our discussion and Ruth's well-deserved win.

It was a slower morning than my first at Toad in the Hole, but that was fine with me. I had a constant running dialogue of what I'd say to Mud when I saw him, and then what I would say to him later from behind Peter's rifle.

The factory lunch crowd began to file in, and I wondered if Mud would show up or not. Part of me wanted to wait on him just to see the look on his face. But I had to be patient. The real payoff would come when I walked into his house with his mother-in-law, already friends with his wife and son.

I watched again from the kitchen with Merle. My heart raced again at the anticipation of seeing him. One by one they entered the dining room. I thought one of the men might be him, but I couldn't be sure. I waited to see how Ruth responded to him. Was there a familiarity between them, or did she treat him as she did all the others. But the true sign was when Aiden came in and didn't sit with him. He didn't even acknowledge him.

I breathed a sigh of relief and joined Ruth in the dining room. I filled water glasses and tended to the diners, knowing that I still had my precious cards up my sleeves.

"I heard you're coming to dinner," Aiden said as I refilled his glass.

"You heard right." I flashed a flirtatious smile and moved on to the next table. The guys Aiden sat with razzed him about liking the new waitress. I turned around in time to see Aiden blush and take a cooling drink of water.

I flirted just enough during lunch to make his tablemates jealous and give him enough hope to tell his parents he was interested in me.

By the time we closed the restaurant, I knew exactly what I was going to do.

"C'mon," Ruth said. "I'll drive."

"I was thinking I would drive myself. You know, in case I want to stay longer." I raised the inflection in my tone so Ruth would interpret it as having something to do with Aiden.

"Well all right then!" Ruth beamed a neon smile and we got on our way.

I used the time alone to prepare myself as much as possible for coming face to face with the monster who took everything from me. I was scared, but I had to be brave.

Be brave. Even when you're scared, be brave.

I wondered what Mud would do when he saw me. I felt secure in assuming he would maintain the front he'd put on for his family as long as they'd known him. But the most important thing would be to keep my cool. I would take my father's gun in my backpack, and the cap bolt gun, just in case Mud went absolutely crazy.

We arrived at 4:15. I anticipated beating Mud and Aiden there, but I guessed the factory let out early on Fridays as well because two cars sat in front of the house already. One was a small, dark blue pickup truck. The other was the big green truck Mud had abducted me in. A shiver ran down my spine at the sight of it.

I eyed Peter's .22-caliber rifle on the floor of the truck before I got out, making sure it would be accessible to me when I needed it. If things played out the way I thought they might, I'd need to get to it quickly.

I met Ruth at the porch and followed her in. As Charlene's mother, she didn't have to knock. She just hollered that we had arrived.

We approached the kitchen and I heard Aiden say, "This is the girl I told you about. I like her, so be nice!"

The voice that replied to him sounded nothing at all like the one I heard call me disgusting names and demand that I tell him how much I enjoyed him raping me. This voice was kind and light, not dark and menacing.

Ruth passed through the doorway into the kitchen with outstretched arms. I followed close behind. This was it, the moment where I took control and where my closure began. I took a deep breath and entered the kitchen. Charlene was at the island cutting some vegetables, Aiden was in the arms of his grandmother, and Mud stood at the sink with his back to me.

"Honey," Charlene called to Mud. "This is Mary."

My heart pounded like drum inside my chest. It was so loud I could barely hear anything else as I waited to see his face again. The last time I laid eyes on him, he had punched me in the face and then tore my clothes from me.

Mud turned around. His happy face morphed into shock and he went white. I pulled out all the bravery my mother instilled in me as I could and stared him square in the eyes.

You hold all the cards, Caroline. You're in control, I reminded myself.

"It's so nice to meet you. I've heard a lot about this Hudson character. Nice to put a face with the name." I extended my hand to shake his, which was the bravest thing I could do. The idea of his skin touching mine repulsed me, but I couldn't let it show.

Mud reluctantly shook my hand. "It's, uh … it's nice to meet you, Mary."

"Dad, you're making things weird," Aiden said to his father, noticing the awkwardness between us.

"Yeah, Hudson! Give the girl her hand back!" Ruth laughed. Mud released my hand and moved behind his wife to the refrigerator. He opened it and stuck his head inside, presumably to lower the heat of nervousness rising in him.

Aiden cozied up next to me in the living room while we waited for the roast to finish. Mud reluctantly joined us after Charlene insisted. I crossed my legs and stared at him as he sat across from me on the couch while Aiden made small talk.

"You know, I never asked where you were from, Mary?"

"I'm from a small town just like Jubilee called Pinewood. Ever heard of it?" I said.

"Nope. I don't get out of Jubilee much, well, at all really," Aiden said.

"What about you Hudson? Ever been to Pinewood?" My gaze fixed on him as he sat there and looked at me across his coffee table, wondering if I was going to reveal his secrets.

"Can't say that I have." He swallowed hard after his lie.

Ruth buzzed into the living room and announced that dinner was ready. Mud bolted from his seat and disappeared into the hall. He was sweating bullets, which meant I had him exactly where I wanted him.

"I'm sorry about my dad," Aiden said. "He's usually not so uptight. I don't know what's going on with him."

"It's okay. Maybe I make him nervous," I suggested.

"Who knows? But he's definitely not acting like himself."

He's not acting like the Mud I know, that's for sure.

"No worries," I replied. "Dinner smells awesome!"

"Oh, you're going to love my mom's roast!"

Aiden put his hand behind my back and guided me to the dining room. Mud sat at the head of the table while Charlene sat to his left closest to the kitchen. She hadn't let her disability limit her. She obviously loved to cook and care for her home. I admired her for not giving up what was important to her.

Aiden sat to his father's right, while I sat next to him and Ruth sat next to Charlene, across from me. It was a quaint, Normal Rockwell setting, with the exception of the rapist sitting at the head of the table.

"Shall we say grace?" Charlene asked. Everyone took hands and Mud, of all people, prayed a blessing over the food. My stomach churned, disgusted that he would have the audacity to speak to God in any capacity. He didn't deserve God's ear. He deserved God's wrath. He was going to get it, too, right after I gave him mine.

"Amen," we said collectively.

"Mary, pass your plate. Let me serve it up for you," Charlene said with an outstretched hand. I passed her my plate and watched her fill it with slices of roast beef, homemade mashed potatoes, and roasted carrots.

"This looks and smells wonderful, Charlene. Thank you so much," I told her.

"It's nothin'." She blushed. "But you're quite welcome." Charlene served everyone else's plates and we all began to eat.

The food tasted as delicious as it smelled. It reminded me of my mother's cooking. She had stopped cooking long before I disappeared. The cancer and its treatment had made it impossible. She had no strength and felt ill so much of the time. I tried and moderately succeeded at some of her recipes, but she was right there to guide me through them. At times I wondered if a Mary Patterson recipe might have brought Dad and me back together after I got home.

My mood turned suddenly very sad. I looked around at Aiden and his mother and grandmother, and my heart broke for the lie they didn't know they were living. The patriarch of their family was not the loving, doting husband and father they thought, but a barbarian. A wolf in sheep's clothing. A rapist. I wanted to scream the truth to them. I wanted to free them. And I would. I would free them by eliminating the monster who sat among them.

My heart turned to Owen. There I was, sitting around a lovely dinner table having a delicious meal with his family, and he was in that little house all alone. Granted, he was probably cooking something amazing, but he was alone. It was wrong that he didn't know the loving kindness of Charlene and Ruth and Aiden. He didn't know the loving kindness of anyone. And then my heart turned to anger.

"Mary?" Ruth said. Her voice brought me back to the moment. "Did you zone out on us?"

"Oh, I'm sorry. Were you talking to me?" I said apologetically.

"I asked if you had any luck tracking down your friend," Ruth said.

I looked at Mud briefly. "Actually, no. But I'm still on the hunt," I told her.

As dinner continued, everyone engaged in small talk but Mud. He ate his meal in silence with his head down like the coward he was. I'd learned that about men like him from the other women in the survivor's group. They weren't mean, aggressive people out in the world, just with the one person they wanted to dominate. That's where they puffed their chests out and let the darkness of their hearts out.

Ruth left around 6:30, claiming that she had to be up very early the next morning because the restaurant opened at 8:00 am. She winked at me on her way out, so I knew what she was up to.

Mud and Charlene excused themselves to the kitchen to wash dishes, leaving Aiden and me alone in the dining room. The awkward silence between us left time for me to feel badly about leading him on. It was only to gain a better footing into their home and give Mud something else to be worried about. How could he ever tell his son to stay away from me without cause?

"Would you like to take a walk?" Aiden asked. He was such a sweet, charming boy. In another life I might actually be interested in him. But right then, my only focus was murdering his father, and that would put a damper on things.

"Sure," I said with a bright smile. I followed Aiden outside and onto the front porch. When we reached the bottom of the steps I turned right, hoping to steer our walk in the direction of the woods and ultimately to Owen's little house. Aiden had other plans.

"This way," he said. I feigned another smile and followed him. The sun had begun to sink, and I worried I'd have to wait another day before I executed the plan that had dominated my mind all day.

"You know, I really shouldn't stay too much longer. I need to be up early to help Ruth at Toad in the Hole tomorrow," I told him.

"Ten minutes. Give me ten minutes and I'll pry myself away." Aiden's eyes were hopeful, which made me feel like a terrible person.

"I think I can spare ten minutes." I smiled flirtatiously and continued walking alongside Aiden. I had only known him two days, but I had such high hopes for him. Hopes that he would never turn out like his father. Hopes that he would one day come to terms with who his father was and be able to move on. That one day he'd be able to forgive me for what I was about to do to his father.

"So, Mary from Pinewood, how long do you think you'll stay in Jubilee?" Aiden asked.

"I don't know," I answered. "Depends how far I get in my hunt for the person I'm looking for."

"You might get farther along in your search if you told us who you were looking for. My dad pretty much knows everyone in town."

"I appreciate your willingness to help, but this is something I have to do on my own." I gave him a faint smile and kept walking. It was quiet for a few minutes before I spoke again.

"So ... you grew up here?" I asked.

"Yep! Moved in when I was a baby, so it's the only house I've ever known," he answered.

"You must have enjoyed some good, old fashioned boyhood out in those woods, then!" I said. Did he know about the little house? "Ever get to explore your dad's *man cave*?"

"Nah. When I was little, Dad tied a rope across the path to tell me how far I could go. He said the path wasn't as clear the further you got and was too dangerous for me," he answered.

"Well, you're not a little boy now," I said with a little too flirtatious of a tone.

Aiden blushed and let out a nervous laugh. "Dad likes to keep his space private, and, well, I haven't explored the woods in a long time."

"Maybe it's time you did." I smiled and changed the subject. "Do you like living in Jubilee?"

"Hmmm…" Aiden began. "If my mother were here I'd tell you I loved it. But since she's not, I'll be completely honest. It's okay. It's a small town with one elementary, middle, and high school. Everyone knows everyone, so there's not a lot of privacy. I mean, I got questioned about you at the factory today. A new face shows up and it stirs the pot," he laughed. "I work at the factory because my dad works there, but I'd really like to leave Jubilee and go to Appleton. The college there has an amazing programming curriculum that I'd love to get into. But … I'm not sure if I can get in now. It might be too late for me."

"So it's been a couple of years since you graduated. So what? If that's what you want to do, you should do it. Don't let anything keep you from following your dream," I told him.

"What about you?" Aiden asked after a moment of thought. "What are you doing with your life besides hunting down some unknown person for unknown reasons?"

"I don't know," I said. "I kinda went through something last year that's made it hard to focus. But all I ever wanted was to work my family's business and—" It occurred to me that I was having an actual conversation with Aiden. One that would draw us closer together. I couldn't do that to him. Hell, I couldn't do that to myself. I was there for one purpose only, and developing a real friendship with Aiden would only cloud my judgment. "You don't want to hear about me."

"No, I do," he said. He took me by the hand as we stopped. "I'd like to know as much as I can about you."

I looked at him and thought maybe there had been a time when Mud wasn't the disgusting excuse for a human being I knew. That maybe the façade he seemed to present to his family was once who he really was. I hoped that whatever happened to Mud would never happen to Aiden. He was kind and sweet and nothing but a gentleman.

Then I thought of Owen again, sitting in that little house in the woods. Alone. All the time, alone. He deserved so much better than that. He deserved the love and hospitality of Charlene. He deserved a nephew like Aiden who would show him what it meant to be a real man. Not Mud's twisted version. I had to save him. My mission turned from avenging the horrors Mud had bestowed on me to rescuing Owen from the darkness of that place. I should have made him come with me that day, and I was going to right that wrong.

I took a cleansing breath to keep from showing the anger building inside of me.

"Oh, Aiden. I'm so sorry, but I can't be that girl right now. Probably not ever," I said. "As much as I like you and your mom and grandmother, I can't stay here. I'm going to go home to Pinewood soon and we'll never see each other again. So, I don't want to lead you to believe that we'll be able to be more than we are right now."

Aiden let out a defeated breath followed by a sweet smile. "I understand. It sucks, but I understand. Walk you back?"

I nodded and Aiden walked me back to my truck. We said our goodbyes and I hugged him, knowing that the next time I saw him it would be after I killed his father.

He watched me pull down the driveway and onto the road before he walked back inside. I was losing daylight, so I had to be quick. I parked next to the abandoned house as I had the day before and pushed my way through the woods with my backpack and Peter's rifle in hand. I made it all the way to Owen's little house and hid on the back side where Mud wouldn't see me. I knew he would go see Owen after Aiden came back in and told him I'd left. It was now or never, and never wasn't an option.

Patiently I waited for Mud to arrive. It wasn't long before I heard the rumbling of an engine and then the slamming of said truck's door. My heart raced.

Be brave. Even when you're scared, be brave.

When the snapping of twigs under footsteps got louder, I stepped out from behind the house with my rifle at the ready.

"Hello, *Mud.*" I let disdain drip from my lips.

"Who the fuck do you think you are? You can't just show up here, come into my house and talk to my wife and son." Mud barked. "And now you're, what, gonna hold me hostage?"

"Are you listening to the words that are coming out of your mouth right now? You kidnapped me and held me captive here for *99 days*. For 99 days I was your personal blow up doll for you to reenact your gross porn with," I yelled. "I'm sure you thought you were flying free when the police couldn't find anyone named Mud in this town. You kept that little nickname between you and the brother no one knows exists."

"What do you want?" he asked. Fear illuminated his eyes, which was exactly what I hoped for.

"What would any girl in my position want? Revenge," I said. "Now open the door."

He opened the door reluctantly and stepped inside. I followed close behind, nudging him with the rifle for added effect.

We entered the living room and found Owen watching television. He stood in shock when he saw me behind his big brother.

"Caroline?" Owen said with surprise.

"Hi Owen. I brought you a gift."

Day 90

It had been a tense five days between Owen and me. I didn't know if it was because he was upset that I had tattled on his brother, or because he knew I was right about Mud and he didn't know how to handle that. We still played backgammon, read, and watched movies. And I taught Owen how to play Uno with doubles and triples the way Mom and I used to play. But if I was going to endure any more time there, or if I had any hope of escaping, I had to make sure things were good between us.

"You've caught on quick," I said to Owen as he laid down two Draw 2 cards. "I've got a massive stack of cards here thanks to you." I chuckled as I drew four cards from the deck.

"I'm sorry. It's mean to make you pick up so many cards," he said. "I won't do it again."

"It's not mean! It's part of the fun!" I told him. "It's a game, Owen. It's okay to play strategically so you win."

"Oh." Owen laid down his second to last card. "Uno."

"Ugh! You are an Uno Jedi Master!" I tossed my cards down and laughed before gathering them all up and shuffling the deck again. "Rematch?"

"I don't know if I want to play anymore right now." Owen's eyes were sad. It was time to address the elephant that had taken up residence in my room.

"You've seemed pretty sad the last few days. Is it because of what happened with Mud?" I asked. No sense in asking if he wanted to talk about it. We had to, and I couldn't let him off the hook.

"I feel ... confused," he admitted.

"About what?" I held my breath and waited to hear if he was going to say what I hoped he would.

He hesitated. "About Mud."

Yes! My efforts to help Owen see Mud's true self were working. Owen had asked him to change his tactic with me and, after a lame attempt, he completely disregarded it. And when Owen asked him about it, he flipped out on both of us. I hated it for Owen, but it had to be done. So did my next course.

"What are you confused about?" I asked. I gave myself points for not highlighting all of the ways Mud treated Owen terribly. He needed to verbalize them for himself.

"I used to think Mud was good and kind, but he's been yelling at me a lot more. He looks like Daddy when he yells." Owen fidgeted with his fingers. "And he started making me watch those movies with him again, even though I told him I never liked them."

Gross.

"Why don't you just tell him that you're not going to watch them?" I asked.

"Mud says that's what makes you a man, and I want to be a man. Except ... I don't want to hurt people like they do in the movies," he answered. "I don't know why Mud wants to hurt you."

"I don't either, Owen. But I think you should be honest with him. You're a grown man and you have a right to say what goes on in your house. If Mud doesn't like it, he doesn't have to come here anymore."

"Oh, I don't think I could kick Mud out. He brings me food and takes care of me." Owen's tone was nervous. The idea of separating himself from his brother frightened him.

"*You* could go get food and anything else you might need," I said. "You're very smart and capable. I bet you could try some new recipes with new foods that you've seen on your cooking shows if you did your own shopping."

His eyes lit up at the suggestion of trying something new. But the light quickly went dark as he remembered his reality.

"I don't know where the grocery store is, and I don't know how to drive a car."

"If you came with me, I could teach you how to drive. You could drive to the grocery store. And you could try new recipes. And you could go and do whatever you wanted." I leaned in with excitement. I wanted him to see the potential his life could have out from under Mud's thumb.

Owen thought for a few minutes while I shuffled and reshuffled the Uno cards. I imagined it was a lot for someone with Owen's mental capacity to process. Everything he knew was being upturned. He had begun to see that Mud was not the person he thought. And I had offered Owen a life Mud would never give him. Still, I could see it weighed heavily on him, and his loyalty to Mud made it difficult for him.

"I ... I don't know," he stuttered.

I would have to force his hand. He needed something to push him over to the other side. My side. The right side. I had an idea, but I couldn't be sure it would work. I had to at least try. If I failed, I'd be in no worse a place.

After we played a four more rounds of Uno, I began setting the stage. I tucked a few cards under the blanket when I cleaned up while Owen got us a snack and another game. I shouldn't have been surprised when Owen returned with a bowl of Goldfish and the backgammon set. I think he liked that it made him feel smart, which was perfect. His confidence needed to be high.

We finished the evening with him having legitimately beaten me three out of five times. I couldn't have asked for a more perfect set up.

"I gotta go. Mud will be here soon," Owen said. He picked up the backgammon set and began to leave.

"Why don't you leave that in here?" I suggested. "We can slide it under the bed and that'll save you from lugging it in here every day."

"I guess that makes sense." Owen handed the game to me and I did as I said I would and slid it under the bed.

"Hey Owen, do you think I could borrow a couple of books? I've been having trouble falling asleep lately and it would really help," I asked.

"Of course. Which ones would you like to borrow?"

"Surprise me!" I told him. Owen smiled and returned a minute later with *The Wizard of Oz* and *Because of Winn Dixie*. "These are perfect. Thank you!"

After Owen took my dinner dishes and said the final goodnights, I pulled everything out and set it on top of the bed. It wasn't much, but if I did it right, it would light the fire that desperately needed to be lit. The one drawback was that I would get burned in the process. I would be okay, though. The blisters from this flame would be worth it.

Day 279

"What are you doing?" Owen asked. He stepped toward us, but I had to cut him off.

"I need you to stay back, Owen," I told him. "I'm here to make right what Mud made so very wrong."

"Aiden's gonna come looking for me if I'm not back soon," he said.

"Oh, you think that's a threat? Even more reason to keep you trapped out here!" I laughed. "I can't wait for Aiden to find your *man cave* and discover what you really do out here. I'm sure the stack of porn in the corner will be super impressive! But I'm glad you brought him up. I just had a lovely walk with him and he's a perfect gentleman. Obviously a nod to what a wonderful *mother* he has. But I'm left wondering something: Why have you left him alone and focused your perversion on Owen?"

"He's only twenty. He's still a boy and … he does just fine with girls," Mud said by way of a pathetic excuse.

"I had just turned eighteen when you took me. Still a girl. So your age requirement doesn't really hold water," I scolded. "You know …

maybe instead of hanging out here, we'll just march right back up to the house."

Mud tried to turn around but I dug my rifle into his back, keeping him in place.

"No! They can't ... he can't ... if Charlene..." he stuttered.

"Yeah. That's a lot of people who don't know the monster you really are. I'm not excited about breaking their hearts because they seem like genuinely nice people, but one day they'll forgive me and move on with the truth of the sadistic maniac they've been living with. Now move." I used the rifle to shove him down the hall to the room where he kept me during those 99 days. The door was ajar.

"Open it," I instructed.

"Owen, do something!" Mud called.

"Shut up! You don't speak unless you're spoken to. *Got it?*" I said, tossing his words back at him. He did as he was told and pushed the door open. "In."

We entered the room and a chill ran down my spine. It had been over nine months but the room looked exactly the same. The bed was disheveled and a stale stench filled the air, presumably from the nasty sheets having never been changed. And on the floor where I had left them were the chain and handcuff.

"Sit down," I told him in a more calm voice. I needed to maintain control. He took two steps toward the bed and turned around. He folded his arms in front of his chest.

"Make me."

Was he really going to try to exert some dominance here?

I chuckled and looked past him, picking a spot on the wall. Then I fired, causing Mud to duck and cover his ears.

"Sit. The fuck. Down." Mud sat while I shifted the bolt handle on the rifle, preparing it to shoot again. "And just so you know: I missed on purpose."

"What do you want? Why would you come back here?" he begged.

"I came back because I'm dead inside and you're still alive. Now pick up the handcuff and latch it on your wrist," I told him. My tone was nothing he'd ever heard from me. It was strong and demanding and everything it needed to be to tell him that I was in charge this time.

"Caroline." Owen's voice came from behind me. I didn't respond until the clicking of the handcuff told me Mud had securely attached himself to the bed the same way I had been. It had to be a disturbing sight for Owen, but he had witnessed much worse. Besides, it was for both of us.

"Now you just sit tight." I glared at Mud and back up out of the room, bumping into Owen as I moved. I pulled the door closed and locked it.

Squeak. Tap. Click.

I turned around and caught Owen's eyes.

"Are you okay?" I asked as I threw my arms around him.

He hugged me back, at first a little hesitantly, but with full force after that. "Yes. I'm okay."

"I'm so sorry for leaving you here. I should have *forced* you to come with me, not taken 'no' for answer," I said. I moved us down the hall into the living room. "But I'm here now and Mud is going to pay for what he did to both of us. Now, where's the key to the door and handcuff?"

Owen went into his tiny kitchen, opened a drawer, and pulled out a key ring with both the pad lock and handcuff keys on them. I held my hand out and he gave them to me.

"Thank you," I said as I shoved them in my pocket.

I took my backpack off and sat on the recliner, laying the rifle on the floor next to me. I pulled out the cap bolt gun and my father's gun and Owen's eyes got wide.

"What are you gonna do, Caroline?" he asked. Nervousness made his voice tremble.

"I haven't decided yet. But come the end of it, he's going to feel the same pain that I did. That *we* did." I tucked both guns back in my bag and took a deep breath. "I need to know what happened after I left."

Owen twisted his mouth while he thought. His eyes shifted as he considered what to tell me.

"It was bad," he said softly.

"Did Mud hurt you again?" I asked. Owen nodded. "And did he take your Hot Wheels away?" Owen nodded again. "How long before he gave them back?" Owen just stared at me. "Owen. How long before he gave them back to you?" He still didn't answer. "Does he still have them?" I asked through gritted teeth. It took a moment, but Owen nodded.

Son of a bitch.

I opened my backpack and pulled out the cap bolt gun and stormed down the hall. I shoved the key into the pad lock and unlatched the door so fast it didn't squeak.

"Your brother does the decent thing and you're still punishing him nine months later? You fucking asshole!" I charged Mud so quickly he didn't have time to think of how to defend himself. He rolled his body into a ball and I jammed the cap bolt gun into his bicep and pulled the trigger. Mud let out a wail so loud I hoped his family would hear it and come running.

"You crazy bitch!" he screamed.

"Yeah, well, you're the one who made me this crazy bitch! Being kidnapped and raped for over three months will do a little damage to one's psyche! Now where are his Hot Wheels?" Mud craned his neck to get a look at the damage I had just done. "Maybe you need a power load in your leg this time to remind you."

"No! No! They're in cellar!" he shouted.

I immediately turned to Owen. "Where's the cellar?"

"It's outside on the other side of the house," he told me.

"Great! Go ahead and get them," I said. Owen didn't move. "It's okay, Owen. They're yours. He had no right to take them from you."

"He won't go down there," Mud interjected.

"Why not?" My glower at Mud was as close to ice as possible.

"Because my parents used to lock him down there," he confessed.

"Holy shit! What is wrong with you people?" I turned to Owen. "It's okay. We'll get them before we leave."

"We?" Mud laughed. "Owen won't go anywhere with you. He's too loyal to me. I saved his life."

"How long are you going to ride that one?' You *ruined* his life! You trapped him here and made him a ghost. No one even knows he exists! What kind of life is that?" I shouted. My face scrunched together at the absurdity of Mud's reasoning. "C'mon, Owen. Your big brother has some thinking to do."

"You can't just leave me in here after you shot me!" he yelled.

"Watch me."

I closed the door again and locked him in.

Squeak. Tap. Click.

My new three favorite sounds.

"You shot him." Owen's expression was unreadable. I couldn't tell if he was happy about it, or upset. I needed to calm down, though. If I was going to be successful in my mission to reveal the true Mud to Owen, there would be a lot more bullshit from Mud. I couldn't let it get to me. I had to keep it together.

"I'm sorry about that. It made me so angry that he took your Hot Wheels away. They mean a lot to you. And what you did that day means a lot to me," I said. "It's not a real gun. It's the gun we use on my family's farm to stun cows before we kill them. We shoot it into the part of their brain that makes it so they don't feel anything."

"Oh." Owen thought for a minute. "You're not going to shoot it into Mud's brain are you?"

I wanted to tell him I wasn't promising anything, but I didn't.

"No. I'm not going to shoot it into Mud's brain."

Owen sat on the couch and rested his elbows on his knees. He had on his thinking face. He did this thing with his mouth and his eyes darted around when he was really trying to figure something out.

"What did you mean?" Owen asked. The expression on my face told him I needed more information to answer his question. "That part when you said no one knows I exist."

How was I to phrase it so that he understood? I couldn't without hurting him, but he had to know.

"It means that Mud's wife and son think he doesn't have a brother. They think that your little house is a place where Mud comes to fiddle with tools and where he keeps his hunting tools," I explained.

I'd never seen Owen's face so sad. He didn't even know the half of it and his heart was already broken in two. It made me want to break my promise of not putting the cap bolt gun to Mud's head and pulling the trigger.

"I need your help with something, Owen," I said. "But it might be hard for you to do."

"What is it?"

"I need you to uncuff Mud, take the chain off, and cuff him to the bed again. Can you do that?" I asked.

"Why do you want to do that? He's already chained up." Owen's expression matched the confusion of his question.

"Right now he has a lot of room to walk around with the chain. I don't want him to have a lot of room," I explained. "Do you think you can help me with that?"

"I don't know."

"Okay. That's okay." I put the gun in the bag and then put my arms through the loops of the backpack. Then I picked up the rifle. "Can you go in first?"

"I can do that," he answered.

We walked to the door and unlatched it.

Tap. Squeak.

I wondered if Mud could hear it as clearly as I had when I was on the other side of that door. I wondered if it scared him like it did me when I first arrived.

I lifted the rifle to my shoulder and Owen turned the doorknob. We entered the room and Mud sat exactly where I had left him. He had torn the sheet and made a tourniquet around his arm.

"How very resourceful of you," I said. "I'd use those sheets sparingly, if I were you. When I'm done with you, there won't be anything left." The same fear that filled me in those first days on that bed oozed from Mud's eyes. I had just gotten there and I already felt so accomplished.

"What do you want? An apology?" Mud's body language still tried to show me he was in control, but his voice betrayed him. The trembling in it matched the trepidation in his eyes.

"An apology? Really? You think after you kept me trapped in this room and raped me for 99 days that all I want is an apology? What I want is for you to pay. At first all I wanted was for you to feel the pain you caused me. But being here again and seeing Owen, what I really want is for you to feel the pain you caused him."

Mud looked at Owen. "Are you going to let her do this to me?" he asked. "I'm your brother, Owen. I've always been there for you. Who is she to us? No one! We're blood, and that runs thicker than anything! I saved you from Mama and Daddy!"

Owen's eyes darted between Mud and me. Mud was confusing him.

"Shut up!" I instructed. "Now, I'm going to give you the key to the handcuffs. You're going to take the chain off and then you're going to loop the cuffs through the headboard and handcuff yourself to the bed. Both wrists. I'm putting you on a short leash. And, in the words of your mother-in-law, if you try anything, I'll shoot your balls off."

I handed the key to Owen, who then handed it to Mud. He stood when he took the chain off and took a step toward me.

"Balls." My one-word reminder was all he needed.

He moved slowly because he only had one good arm, but that was okay. I could wait. When he completed his task, he sat with his back against the wall and his hands cuffed to the scrolling in the middle of the headboard.

"Owen, can you come stand over here next to me?" I asked.

"Don't listen to her, Owen! You need to help me here!" Mud demanded.

"Didn't anyone ever tell you that you catch more flies with honey than vinegar? See, I *asked* Owen if he'd come stand next to me. All you ever do is order him around. I'm a breath of fresh air, Mud." I stared him down to the point of willing fire to shoot from my eyes. I put the rifle down and pulled the cap bolt gun from my bag. There were no bullets like in the rifle since it was just for rendering the brains of cows senseless. I determined Mud would last longer with a few cap bolt holes in him than shots from the rifle. "Owen, would you like to know the truth about Mud and your family?"

He looked at Mud and then at me ... at Mud then back at me. "Yes."

"She doesn't know shit! She's gonna make up lies so you'll want to leave here," Mud whined.

"I don't have to make anything up. First of all, he remembers exactly what you did to him right before I escaped. And I don't even want to know what you did to him after. Second, I've been talking to your Charlene and Ruth. They've given me enough information to sink you with Owen. So," I said, "we're going to play a little game. I ask a question. For every wrong or dodgy answer, I pull the trigger. Got it?"

"Fuck you!"

"I'll take that as a yes," I declared with as much sass as possible. "Shall we begin?"

Day 91

I hardly slept that night. I kept waking up to make sure everything was still where I had left it. I didn't want anything falling behind the bed. All the evidence needed to be out where Mud would see it.

Already awake when Mud's steps approached the door, I opened The Wizard of Oz to the middle and laid it on my chest, pretending to have fallen asleep. The book wouldn't be what cinched things, though.

Tap. Squeak.

The door opened and Mud entered. I sat up and let the book fall for effect.

"What the hell is all this?" Mud barked.

"I, uh … I was just reading. Owen gave me some books to help me sleep," I stuttered.

"Owen!" Mud yelled. His eyes were as wide as saucers when he joined us.

"I'm sorry, Owen," I said, indicating to the open backgammon game. "I was practicing. You've gotten so good that I just—"

"What is she talking about, Owen?" Anger painted Mud's face, and rudeness dripped from his lips.

"Uh ... um..." Owen couldn't find the words. I felt badly that I had set him up, but it was all I knew to do to reveal the monster inside of Mud to him.

"Uh, um ... is that all you've got, boy?" Mud turned to Owen and pushed him. "You've been in here playing games and, what, reading books? Have you even fucked her once?" Mud pushed him again.

"Stop, Mud. You're hurting me." Owen's voice was small, but I was proud that he spoke up.

"Oh, I haven't even gotten started yet! You ungrateful little shit!" Mud grabbed Owen's shirt with his left hand and slapped him repeatedly upside his head. Owen's head dropped to the side. He raised his hands up to try and stop Mud, but it was useless. Mud was bigger and stronger than he was.

"Mud! Please! Stop!" Owen begged. It only seemed to fuel Mud's rage. He continued to slap Owen's head and shake him by the fist full of shirt in his hand.

"I try to help you become a man, and you don't appreciate it! I take care of you! Make sure you have everything, and this is how you repay me? I backed off because you asked me to! Because you said you wanted her to yourself! You little shit! You're as stupid and Mama and Daddy said you were!"

Mud eventually let go and Owen fell on the floor into a crumpled mess. He pulled his knees to his chest and engulfed his head with his arms. He sobbed as only someone who had just been cut down by the only person he trusted could be.

"You stay down there!" Mud instructed. Owen lifted his head and looked at me. I mouthed the words *I'm sorry*.

"You." Mud stared me down and took a deep breath. "I'm going to enjoy getting back to this more than once a day."

"No, please, don't," I begged. I backed into the corner and curled up in a ball. It only seemed to excite him more.

"Oh, yeah! Gimme some fight!" He reached across the bed and grabbed my ankles with both hands. He yanked me to the side of the bed. I kicked and screamed and shouted 'no' more times than I could remember. He plastered a disturbing smile across his face.

"Owen! Help me!" I yelled. I looked over at Owen rocking back and forth, still hiding his face from the terror in front of him.

"He ain't gonna help you! He's a stupid little pussy. You're all mine now!" Mud stripped me of my pants and pulled my shirt off with such force that I thought my head was going to snap. He pushed me down on the bed, then he grabbed my thighs and lifted me up, slamming himself into me in one motion. I let out a yell and cried for the first time in months while Mud raped me.

"No! No!" was all I could manage through my wailing.

Mud pulled out and grabbed my arm to sit me up. Then he demanded something he had never had before. "Suck it." His words were like fingernails on a chalkboard.

"No!" I yelled.

He grabbed the back of my head, a fist full of hair between his fingers, and jerked my head back.

"I said, suck it. And if I feel your teeth for one second, we'll do it all over again."

Tears had flooded my eyes so much that I could barely see. They were filmy and it made everything in front of me hazy, including Mud's disgusting penis.

He took ahold of my head just above my ears and I reluctantly opened my mouth. He glided himself in and over my tongue. I immediately gagged, but that didn't stop him. He rocked his hips back and forth, sliding himself in and almost out of my mouth, groaning while I cried harder and harder.

"Yeah, like that! That's good!" he moaned. I prayed to God he wouldn't come in my mouth. By some miracle, he tired of that and yanked himself out of my mouth. I gagged and coughed while he stood me up and bent me over. I spit out as much of the nastiness of him as I could before he thrust himself into me again.

He was rougher than he'd ever been. It wasn't just about dominating me and getting off. He was angry. Angry that Owen had deceived him and cut his time with me. Angry that Owen had asserted some dominance of his own and that he listened to it. He was proving a point, showing Owen who was in control.

Mud lasted longer than he normally did, obviously charged by his aggression. When he finally did finish, he didn't pull out. Instead, he came inside me for the first time. I was shredded to my very core.

I lifted my arm for him to release me for my shower, but it hung in midair. I turned and sat on the edge of the bed, pulling the sheet up to cover myself. I extended my arm again.

"No shower for you today. I'm back in charge and I'll let you know when you get to take a shower," Mud buckled his pants and turned to Owen. "Stand up." Owen shuddered at the sound of Mud's voice. "It's okay, little brother. If you ain't gonna have her, I will." Mud's angry tone had turned passive. He acted as if he hadn't just physically and verbally beat the shit out of his brother. He reached down and took Owen by the arm, helping him stand. "You can play all the games with her you want during the day, and I'll play *my* games with her every morning and night."

Owen looked at me briefly as Mud pushed him out the door. I had no words for the traumatic scene he and I had just endured. Was it worth it, revealing our secret to Mud? Only time would tell.

Day 279

Mud sat huddled in the corner of the bed like a wounded dog because that what he was: a dog. No. Calling him a dog was too good. Dogs were kind, sweet, loving animals. Mud was wild and vicious.

"First question," I said. "Were there other girls?"

"No," he said quickly.

"Owen? Care to weigh in on that?" I asked. Mud shot daggers at Owen and unsuccessfully tried to shake his head so I wouldn't see it. "Owen?"

"There was one other girl a long time ago," he finally said.

I cocked my head at Mud. "That was such an easy one, too." I lifted the cap bolt gun and stepped closer to Mud. He curled up against the wall protectively, exactly how I did when he came for me. He tried to swat me away, but I got close enough to get a good shot in his thigh. Blood dripped from the muzzle where the pin pushed into Mud's flesh.

"You bitch!" Mud screamed.

"Tell the truth and I won't have to shoot you. Keep lying and I'm going to use the rifle. Now, question number two," I said. "What happened to that girl?" Mud stayed silent and looked away. "Owen? Do you know what happened to her?"

Owen shook his head. "She was here for a while, and then I got up one day and Mud said she had to go."

"Did you let her go?" I directed my question to Mud again.

"No," he finally said. "I came in one morning and she had broke the mirror in the bathroom and sliced her wrists in the shower."

I shook my head in disgust. *That poor girl's family is still wondering where she is.*

"Why me? What were you doing in Pinewood?" I pushed the issue of the girl aside and returned to find answers for Owen.

"That's two questions," Mud said smugly.

"Really? You want to be sassy right now? Because I'm happy to put another hole in you just for being a dick. Answer my question."

"Fine. I was looking for someone … for Owen," he said.

"A girl. You were looking for a *gift* for Owen." Mud nodded. "So why me?"

"You look like the girl in Owen's favorite movie," Mud explained.

I turned to Owen. "Is that true? Do I look like one of those girls?" I was mortified that I would remind anyone of a sleazy porn star.

Owen looked embarrassed and dropped his head as he nodded.

"To be fair," Mud began. Did he even know what that meant? "The only one he liked had all that gentle, first time shit in it."

"That's because he's not a monster like you," I barked back at him. "But since we're talking about Owen, he deserves some truth, too." I turned my attention to Owen and changed my tone. "Do you want to know the truth about why Mud has kept you here? About your parents?"

Owen looked at Mud with an expression I'd never seen on him before. He was finally getting angry with his older brother. The seeds that I had planted all those months ago had taken root, and the pieces of everything were all suddenly in front of him and he desperately needed them put together.

"Yes. I wanna know why you kept me here, Mud," Owen declared.

"Owen." Mud's tone changed from aggressive to one of placation. "I kept you here to keep you safe."

"Lie." I stepped forward jammed the cap bolt gun into Mud's shoulder as I pulled the trigger. After I punctured his arm and leg, he was too occupied with tending to those wounds that he didn't have the strength to fight me off.

"Fuck!"

"Stop lying! Tell. Him. The truth!"

Owen leaned over to whisper in my ear. Mud's moaning from the pain would keep him from hearing him anyway. "Is Mud gonna die from those shots?"

"Not unless I shoot him in the brain, and I won't do that. They aren't bullets in this gun. The pin is making him hurt really bad, though," I whispered back. It was mostly true. I didn't know exactly what would happen if you shot a person with a cap bolt gun, but I was getting my desired effect, and that's all I cared about.

"Oh, okay," Owen replied.

"Fine," Mud said after he caught his breath. "I kept you here because Mama and Daddy told me to. They never told anyone about you, so neither did I."

"Why didn't they tell anyone about him?" I challenged. He looked ashamed for about half a second.

"He was born at home, here in this room, but there were complications. The cord was wrapped around Owen's neck and he came out all blue. The doc was able to revive him but said that he'd have a lot of mental problems. Mama and Daddy took him to the hospital in Avon City where they ran a bunch of tests on him. They confirmed that parts of his brain don't work right and that he'd never be normal. They tried to put him up for adoption but no one would take him once they saw his medical records," Mud explained.

"How on earth do you keep a child hidden from the whole town?" I asked.

"Jubilee wasn't even *this* big back then, so keeping him hidden wasn't a problem."

"Let me get this straight. Your parents were so backwoods ignorant that they were embarrassed to have a child with some kind of mental disability?" I asked.

"No. That just made the situation worse." Mud's eyes darted between Owen and me.

"What situation?" Owen asked.

"Mama had an affair and Owen was the result." Mud couldn't even look his brother in the eye when he revealed the secret he'd been holding in.

A pensive hush came over the room as Owen took in what his brother had just said. I wanted to ask him if he understood, but by the look on his face, it seemed to be coming together in his mind.

"So, Daddy ain't my daddy?" he asked, surprising me with his understanding.

"No," Mud said simply.

Owen thought for another moment. "How come you never told me?"

"When you were born, they made me promise not to tell," Mud answered.

"You could have told him after they were gone," I interjected.

"He had already been kept hidden that long. How was I supposed to bring him out to the town after 13 years? Besides, he had a good setup here."

"Bullshit!" I said before I shot him in the other shoulder. The sadness that engulfed Owen was overwhelming me.

"I'm the one who kept him alive! Mama and Daddy put him out here when he was eight! I played with him! I brought him food and clothes! The time I spent with him was the only real interaction he had with anyone! Mama and Daddy only brought him pain! They couldn't even look at him without calling him names or beating the shit out of him!" It was the first time I saw anything genuine in Mud. He really had been there for Owen when their parents weren't. "To Daddy, he was the reminder that Mama had cheated on him. To Mama, he was her punishment."

"And to you?" I asked. "Who was he to you?"

Mud's face was a mixture of physical and emotional pain. "He was the one who made them quit beating me."

And there it was. I didn't know much, but I knew Mud was a textbook example of how the sins of the father are passed on to the son.

"After your parents were gone, you could have introduced him to Charlene and Aiden. To the world. You could have given him a *good* life," I said with contempt.

"Look at him. He's always going to be seven years old. What kind of life would it be for him out there?" Another lame excuse.

"You think this has been a great life for him here? He's been excluded from every experience a person is supposed to have. He never got to go to school. Never got to make friends or play on a playground. He's never been outside of these woods! It would be a wonderful world where he could be loved and cared for," I countered.

"I love my brother. It might not look like what you think it should, but I do," Mud said defensively. "When our parents were gone—after I killed them to keep Owen safe, by the way—I continued to take care of him and give him everything he needed."

Owen stood next to me and tried to absorb everything. It had to be overwhelming and confusing for him. The man he thought was his father wasn't. No one knew he existed because Mud and his parents were embarrassed by his mental deficiencies. Owen didn't understand a lot of things, but he understood that.

He left the room and I assumed he needed a few moments to gather his thoughts. I could have never predicted what would happen when he returned.

"You treated me the way Mama and Daddy did," Owen said as he returned with Peter's rifle in his hand. "And you told me they didn't really love me. That means you don't love me."

"Now, hold on a minute, Owen. Don't let her make you all confused," Mud said in between winces. "She marched in here and started stirring up a pot that didn't need to be disturbed."

"Her name is Caroline and she's my friend. She wouldn't be here if you hadn't brought her here in the first place. You hurt me and you hurt Caroline," Owen said strongly. There was a fire in Owen's eyes I'd never seen before. He lifted the rifle that had been at his side. I watched, silently waiting to see what he was going to do and if I needed to act.

Before I realized what was happening, Owen took hold of the rifle like a baseball bat and charged Mud. He swung at him over and over again. Mud lowered his head between his arms protectively, but that didn't keep the handle of the rifle from making contact with his head. Blood splattered on the walls and added to the stains already caused by the wounds I had inflicted on Mud.

Mud cried out in pain, and Owen took the handle of the gun and butted it into his side repeatedly. Soon, Mud stopped moving. He winced and cried, so I knew he was still alive, at least for now.

Owen collected himself and straightened his back. He walked toward me and then leaned the rifle against the wall by the door. He turned and glared at the near lifeless body of his brother.

"I want my Hot Wheels back."

Day 99

The last seven days were harder than the previous 92. Mud had become more aggressive with both Owen and me. He arrived earlier in the morning and took longer, moving me around more and trying new things. Of all the things he tried, I just couldn't stomach his need for oral. I gagged every time, and every time he threatened to kill me if I threw up on him. On two occasions he raped me twice before going to work. I barely had time to catch my breath before he was ordering me to tell him to do it again.

I hated every second of it, and many times I prayed he would just kill me. But somehow, hearing his treatment of Owen became even more heartbreaking. I was mentally stronger than Owen. I could reason out Mud's atrocities and call them for what they were: evil. But Owen trusted Mud. He believed everything Mud told him. For Mud to have physically and verbally beaten him so badly the day he discovered our secret was one thing. But every day after, Mud entered the house and made a loud showing of his dominance over Owen.

"Good morning, stupid," he'd yell when he entered. And when he left, "Try not to be stupid today. I know that might be hard, but give it your best shot."

Owen still came in and kept me company during the day. We read and played games, and had watched a couple of movies, so everything with us was as back to normal as it could get. The pressure was off at the end of the day, though. There was no need to make sure we were done with our game or movie before Mud got there. We had nothing to hide. Mud even waited for us to finish what we were doing once.

To make up for Mud's increased violence with me, Owen had upped his game on what he made me for dinner. He graduated from peanut butter and jelly to nicer things like soup and grilled cheese. He was honestly the kindest person I had ever known. It broke my heart for him to be treated so heinously. It would be an injustice to anyone, but even more so because of Owen's deficiencies.

"Turn over!" Mud barked at me. I flipped from my back to my knees as quickly as possible. Any delay would mean a harder pull of my hair once I was on all fours. He had become a fan of that and I was beginning to have a near constant headache.

"Say it!" he demanded. I rolled my eyes, grateful he couldn't see my face. It added insult to injury to make me declare such disgusting things to him. When I didn't respond fast enough, he slapped my hip with all his might, leaving a stinging sensation rolling through me. "Say it, bitch!"

I took a breath and complied. "You feel so good," I said with no emotion. "Don't stop."

He groaned and thrust into me a few more times before he was done. Once again, as he had for the previous seven days, he came inside me.

I turned around and held my cuffed wrist out for him. "Can I please shower today?" It was degrading that I even had to ask.

"You showered two days ago. Maybe tomorrow ... if you're good." With that, Mud left me sitting on the bed, tears waiting to fall until he was gone.

Squeak. Tap. Click.

I sobbed uncontrollably. I was never going home. Any thoughts I had that my grand plan of getting Mud to reveal himself to Owen would lead to anything were streaming down my face. They would dry up and never be seen again.

"Try not to be stupid today, Owen!" Mud yelled as he began to leave. "I know that'll be hard, but do your best." Mud slammed the door behind him.

I did my best to stop crying and took a deep breath. I stood up to go use the bathroom when I heard the *tap, squeak* of Owen's arrival. He was early. I sat back down so the fluid Mud had left in me wouldn't run down my leg. The white undershirt Owen had given me was too big and covered me completely whether I stood or sat.

Owen charged in quickly. "You have to go *now*," he said excitedly.

Stunned, I stared at him like a deer caught in headlights. "What?" I couldn't believe my ears. "You're letting me go?"

"Yes," Owen said softly.

"Why?" I asked. The real question was, why was I wasting time asking questions?

"Mud is not a good person. I'm sorry I made you stay here with me," he answered.

Ecstatic, I jumped up and pulled my pants on, letting the fluid that was flowing out of me soak into the material. I didn't even care. I was going home.

Owen met me and released the cuff from my wrist. I looked around on the floor but couldn't find my shoes.

"Where are my shoes?" I asked as I fluttered around looking for them.

"I don't know, but you need to hurry so you'll be far, far away by the time Mud gets home tonight," Owen said.

I started toward the door, but then stopped and turned.

"Come with me, Owen. Come with me. It'll be just like with Ariel. You can come with me to a place where you're free to be you. We have a big house and lots of land. More land than you've ever seen!" I implored him. "Come with me and you'll never have to be alone ever again!"

Owen caught my eyes and I could see he was considering my offer. He didn't want to be there anymore. He had experienced the evil inside Mud. He knew in his heart that wasn't how you were supposed to treat someone you loved, but he couldn't reconcile leaving Mud. His ties to him were too strong.

"I can't," he finally said.

I threw my arms around him like I had the first time he tried to let me leave. Tears fell from my eyes. I didn't want to leave him in that terrible place. Owen was kind and loving, and he deserved the same in return. I felt I was betraying him somehow by leaving.

I took him by his shoulders and reiterated my invitation. "Are you sure? I really want you to come with me. I don't want to leave you here with him. He's going to be very angry when he finds out what you've done."

"I know. But I have to do the right thing. He may be mad, but he'll stop being mad after a while and then we'll be okay again," he said.

I studied Owen's face. His eyes were stronger than they had been before. And, while I didn't like leaving him, I suddenly felt like he might be okay. If he could stand up and be strong now, then maybe he could be strong all the time.

"Promise me something," I said. "Be brave. Even when you're scared, be brave." Owen nodded and I gave him the best smile I could. I left the bedroom and headed for the door when Owen stopped me.

"Wait!" he said. Owen ran into his room and returned with a denim jacket and a pair of sneakers. "Here, take these. And remember, don't take the path. You have to go through the woods." I nodded as I put the jacket and shoes on and then bolted out of the house. I inhaled the fresh air into my lungs and became overwhelmed with freedom.

To my left was the path Owen explicitly told me to avoid, so I took off to the right, grateful for the jacket and shoes in the cool air. Both were too big on me, but I didn't care.

I made my way through the woods, leaving Owen's little house in the distance. I had no idea where I was going. Away from the horror I had lived for 99 days was all I needed.

I ran as fast as I could, my lungs burning and my head pounding from the cold air I inhaled. I didn't look back. Not once. I knew no one was following me, but I didn't want to look back and be wrong. Mud had surprised us by coming home early before. There was nothing to say that he hadn't decided to call in sick and have another go at me. I couldn't risk looking back and stumbling into a tree, either. Time was valuable and I didn't want to do anything that would slow me down.

As I ran, I discovered the problem with the beautiful blanket of fallen leaves: they covered the rocks and dips in the terrain. I fell more times than I could count. I did my best to keep Owen's shoes from falling off. I tied them as tight as I possibly could, but they still flopped on my bare feet.

I found a cluster of rocks and fallen trees and scurried inside. I tried to slow my breathing, make the burning in my chest and the throbbing in my sinuses stop so I could ready myself for more running. I didn't rest for too long. I couldn't waste time.

The sun had risen, but it was still low in the sky. The light streamed through the barren trees, blinded me at times. I held my hand above my eyes like a visor to block the sun, but it was too late. I didn't see the gully ahead of me. I dropped like a lead balloon and rolled into the gully with full force. My arms flailed and scraped against rocks and dead branches, and when I finally stopped, I face planted, with my ribs landing hard on a cluster of rocks. And Owen's shoes were nowhere to be seen.

After I caught my breath, I rolled over as gingerly as I could. My arms and legs were scraped, but otherwise fine. I didn't know if I had broken any ribs. I felt my face and saw blood on my hand when I pulled it away. The gash on my cheek seemed pretty big, and the stinging on my lip told me I had split it.

I rested longer than I should have. I didn't know how far I had to go before I would find civilization or if Mud was out looking for me. It was unlikely, but I couldn't rule it out. So I got up and continued. I stopped running. With my new injuries I had to be careful. Another fall could render me unable to walk, and then I would be left to die out there.

I don't know how long I walked, and I certainly had no idea how far. I could only gauge the time by the sun. It had moved significantly, so I put myself at having walked for around two hours through those woods when I finally reached a road.

It was your typical, two-lane, backwoods road that wound through a lot of "middle of nowhere" places. My feet were sore and scratched from walking barefoot. They were caked with dirt, too. Oddly enough, walking on the side of the road was a welcome change from the forest floor.

I pulled Owen's jacket around me tightly for warmth. It wasn't incredibly cold outside, but to have been out in the elements as long as I had, I was feeling frigid. I continued walking along the road for I don't know how long. Another hour maybe? I came across an abandoned general store from back in the day. It had a porch and covering, so I stopped and sat. I pulled my knees to my chest and leaned against the side of the store. My head felt heavy, so I folded my arms on my knees and rested my head.

I sat there, dirty and disheveled and happier than I had been in 99 days. I didn't know how far I would have to walk before I made it to anywhere that could get me home to my parents in Pinewood, but I didn't care. I was out from under Mud's thumb, and that was all that mattered.

When I felt rested enough to stand and begin my journey again, a single-axle semi truck rounded the corner I had come from. Without my prompting, it stopped, and so did my heart. Was Mud behind the wheel? I stepped back until I hit the wall of the general store. The man rolled down the passenger side window and leaned over to speak to me. I let my heart beat again when I saw it wasn't Mud. The driver had long, light brown hair and a beard.

"Miss? You okay?" he called out to me. "You need some help?"

I stared up at him, unable to speak. I didn't know what to do. My body trembled from fear, cold, and pure exhaustion. I had a very strong case of stranger-danger. Did I answer him? Was it safe to get into his truck? I didn't know where I was, and I needed to get to the nearest big city as quickly as I could.

I gathered all the bravery I could and nodded.

"You need help?" he clarified. I nodded again. He got out of the truck and rounded the cab. Getting an up close view of my state, he worked to reassure me. "I'm Charlie. I'm not going to hurt you." Nodding seemed to be the only thing I could do.

Charlie opened the passenger door and helped me in. It was difficult because I had to climb. The movements highlighted my sore muscles and wounded ribs.

"Do you know where you're going?" he asked.

"Pinewood," I managed as I stared out the window.

"I'm headed to Mason, which is about an hour from here. There's a real good hospital there, and by the looks of ya, you need one,"

Charlie said. I nodded again and watched the world go by through the window.

While time seemed to stand still in that little room at Owen's house, the hour to Mason flew by. Charlie helped me from the cab of his truck and into the emergency room of Mason Medical Center.

"Excuse me, miss?" he called out to the receptionist behind the counter. "I found her out on Saw Mill Road in Pollack County, about an hour from here. I don't know her name or what happened to her, but she's beat up pretty bad. I think something awful happened," he said.

"Okay," the woman behind the desk said. She picked up the phone and called for someone to come. A moment later a nurse arrived with a wheelchair. Charlie helped me sit.

"You take care of yourself, okay?" he said to me. He began to walk away but I grabbed his arm.

"Thank you," I said. Relief flooded my body and tears made trails in my dirtied face.

"You got it, darlin'."

With that, my semi-driving angel walked out through the sliding doors, and I was wheeled into an exam room.

The nurse helped me onto the exam table and began to get my vital signs. She helped me remove Owen's jacket and rolled the blood pressure machine next to me. Before she did anything else, she looked at me sweetly and attempted to ascertain who I was and what had happened to me.

"I'm Kendall. I'm gonna take care of you, get you examined and cleaned up, okay?" she said. "Now, can you tell me your name and what happened?"

I looked at her and uttered the words I never thought I'd get to say.

"My name is Caroline Patterson. I was kidnapped from Pinewood 99 days ago."

Day 280

Owen and I sat in the living room of his little house for hours, completely silent. Occasionally Mud would break the silence with a pained wail or a curse. The clock had long passed midnight and no one had come looking for him. They most likely thought he had gotten caught up in whatever project he was working on in his man cave and had left him to it. I had honestly hoped Aiden would come to find him. He needed to know the truth. He needed to know the disgusting low-life his father really was. The sooner he knew that, the sooner he'd be able to move on with his life in the truth.

I watched Owen process what had happened and wondered how he was coping. He had been completely silent and eerily calm since he finished beating the shit out of his brother. I wasn't sure how *I* felt about what had happened. I had set out to end Mud so I could have closure, but had found so much more.

"Owen?" I finally said. "Are you okay?"

He looked up at me. "Yes," he said. "I shouldn't have hurt him, but I'm okay."

"What do you want to do?" I asked.

Owen thought for a moment before answering. "We should get him some help."

"Okay. We can do that." I picked up my phone to call for help, knowing that Owen and I would be held responsible for our actions. I had no idea how it would play out, but I was willing to take whatever came at me. I had survived everything Mud put me through. I could survive anything.

I pulled up my contacts and called the only person I knew who could help.

"Hello?" a sleepy voice answered. "Caroline?"

"I'm sorry to call so late, Officer Moore," I said.

"It's fine. Are you okay?" she asked.

"Yeah. I'm okay," I told her. "I have that lead you need."

A little over three hours later, Officer Moore and her team converged on Charlene's house. I waited outside to greet them, knowing their arrival would be unsettling for Charlene and Aiden. On my instruction, they called for an ambulance. Mud was going to need one.

Some officers waited with Charlene while I walked Officer Moore back to Owen's house. She didn't ask any questions along the way. She simply waited to see what I had to show her.

When she walked in, Owen stood to greet her.

"This is Owen," I said. "I'm going to have to explain him in a minute." They shook hands and then I took her to the back room. She noted the latch on the door was just as I had described. Then I opened the door to the bedroom where a bloodied, yet still alive, Mud lay curled up on the bed. "And this is Mud." I identified him as my abductor and rapist.

"You've got a lot to explain," Officer Moore said.

"Yes. I do."

The ambulance arrived and took Mud away, an officer accompanying him since he would technically be in custody. I spent the next hour explaining everything that had happened, and all that I had discovered. From creating my own 10-mile radius to finding Ruth at Toad in the Hole to stumbling upon Mud's house to the girl who killed herself in the shower. I told her about how the police would have never found Mud because no one but Owen called him that. I explained the heartbreaking truth behind why Owen was kept a secret. And I told her about how Owen saved my life. Not just on the day he let me escape, but every day.

By the time the sun rose, Officer Moore had questioned both Owen and me thoroughly, and we told her everything.

"I understand that you have to do your job," I told her. "I know what we did was legally wrong. But he had it coming."

"I should probably arrest both of you," she said. "But I'm pretty sure the victim isn't going to press charges. And once we match his DNA to your rape kit, that'll be it for him." Officer Moore stood. "I'm glad this over for you."

"Me, too." Although it wasn't over just yet.

I took Owen by the hand and walked him outside and up the forbidden path to the big house. Charlene and Aiden were outside. Officer Moore was explaining the situation to them. The shocked expressions on their faces were genuine. They had no idea Mud had been living a double life. They shook their heads in denial and I heard Aiden yell "no" at Officer Moore. She spoke some more and I imagined she was confirming that the evidence was there. Everything I had described nine months before was accurate to what she had found. If she could have, Charlene would have collapsed to the ground. Aiden knelt beside her. They held each other and cried.

We stopped about 10 yards from them. I didn't want to disturb them, but Aiden looked up at me and drew his mother's attention to us. With light feet, we moved toward them. Their eyes were sorrowful and compassionate.

"I am so, so sorry," Charlene said. "It's just so hard to believe."

"He kept it hidden well. There was no way for you to know," I said. "What happened to me was awful, but it only lasted 99 days. What he did to Owen lasted his whole life." I put my hand behind Owen and presented him to Charlene and Aiden. "This is Owen. Mud, uh, Hudson's brother."

They took him in and Charlene began to cry again. "Hello, Owen. I'm Charlene and I'm very pleased to meet you." She extended both her hands and wrapped them around his. "You are *very* welcome in this family."

Owen looked at me and I smiled softly at him.

"I'm Aiden. I guess I'm your nephew," he said.

"I always wanted to know you. Mud said that you wouldn't like me very much because I'm not smart," Owen said to them.

"Well," Charlene began. "Hudson doesn't speak for us. You're family, and like I said, you are welcome here."

"Caroline?" Officer Moore called to me.

"Oh, yeah, my name isn't Mary," I said.

"Yes. Officer Moore explained that," Charlene replied.

"I'm sorry I lied to you. I never expected to find such wonderful people. In fact, the more I got to know you, the angrier I got. Please know that I'm truly sorry for what happened to Hudson." Charlene nodded and I left Owen standing with them while I met with Officer Moore.

"You'll need to come in tomorrow and give an official statement," she said. "I'll send someone back out here to get Owen's."

"Tell them to go slow with him and be patient. He has trouble gathering his thoughts and he gets confused. If it's too much for him, I can come back and help him," I said.

"I'll let you know if we need you," she answered.

I watched Owen interacting with Charlene, Aiden, and the now-present Ruth. They were gentle with him like I knew they would be. He was timid, but warming up to them well. They were all he ever wanted: a family. It was sad and beautiful to watch at the same time.

"Um ... hi Ruth," I said. Ruth flung her arms around my neck and held me tight.

"If everything they're tellin' me is true, I couldn't be more sorry, darlin'!" she said. "I promise we had no idea he was such a monster."

"Mama!" Charlene said sharply.

"Well, he was! Ain't no use in pretending this girl came all the way out here on a whim and randomly picked Hudson to tell wild lies about!" Ruth took me by the shoulders. "What can we do?"

There was nothing anyone could do to erase what Mud had done to me. My abduction and rape would always be a part of my history. In time it wouldn't hurt as much. And one day I'd hopefully be able to use my healing to help someone the way Donna had helped me. I would have a lot to discuss with Dr. Wendy and the group when I got home.

But what about Owen? How would he recover? How would he heal?

"Take care of Owen. He's your family and he needs you," I said.

"Of course," Charlene said.

"You're okay with me not coming with you?" Owen asked. He was so sweet to think of me in that moment.

"Yes. You all have a lot of healing to do. And, well, we need our family for that. Which is why I need to go home." I took Owen's hand in mine. "You're going to be just fine. They're going to take real good care of you."

Owen hugged me tight. "I missed you when you left the first time. I'm going to miss you even more now."

"Me, too. But the good news is that we can stay in touch this time. Okay?"

"Okay," Owen nodded.

I gave a tight-lipped smile to the family of the man who had destroyed my life and walked away.

An officer was kind enough to drive me to my truck. Once inside, I let out the breath I had been holding for nine months and cried massive tears. Tears of sorrow. Tears of joy. And tears of relief. I could never say I did the right thing by hunting Mud down. But I would never regret doing it. If I hadn't, Owen would still be imprisoned in the duty and loyalty Mud had masked as love and security. And who knows how many other girls Mud would have hurt? Mud was a sick, sick man and he needed to be removed from society.

When all the tears had fallen, I was halfway home. I did something I hadn't done in months: I turned the radio on. Music filled the space, the man's voice singing about the ghosts we knew flickering from view and living a long life. That was me now. Mud was my ghost and he was disappearing. It was Owen, too. We could now both live a long and happy life.

I stopped to see Mom before I went home. The leaves from the tree had almost all fallen and I had to brush them off and away from her headstone before I sat.

"Hi, Mom," I said. "I'm not sure where to start, although if you're looking down on me you already know I did something really crazy and mostly stupid. It won't be easy to move forward, but I can now that Mud is going to be brought to justice." I thought of what to say next and came up empty. "Actually … I guess all I wanted you to know is I'm okay now. And … I was brave. Even when I was scared, I was brave."

Day 350

I drove down to the end of the driveway to get the mail. It was the usual solicitation from farming suppliers and a few bills. But mixed among them I found a letter from Owen. I smiled so wide I felt it in my ears.

It had been just over two months since that fateful night in his little house. Mud was arrested and charged with a litany of offenses against both Owen and me, as well as against the girl he had taken before me. He identified her and told them where he buried her body. He spent three weeks recovering in the hospital before he was moved to the jail in Pollack County. Officer Moore didn't think there would be a trial. She said the evidence against him was so airtight, he'd take whatever they gave him. That was good. The last thing Owen and I wanted to do was relive the horrors Mud had subjected us to in front of a judge and a group of strangers.

Officer Moore couldn't ignore the night of terror we rained down on Mud, so she suggested a psychological evaluation for both of us. Dr. Wendy and the doctor Owen saw diagnosed both of us with PTSD. The judge read our files and dismissed all the charges against us.

Owen and I began working to rebuild our lives. Well, I was rebuilding. Owen was pretty much starting from scratch.

Charlene took Owen under her wing as only she could. He had been learning what it meant to be genuinely loved and cared for since the second they met him. He had taken to writing me letters as his handwriting and spelling had improved. I'd only received a few so far, but they were the highlight of my day.

I hopped into the truck and drove back up to the house. I grabbed all the mail and took a seat at the top of the porch steps. I wasted no time in tearing Owen's letter open. To my surprise, it was typed.

Dear Caroline,

Look! I'm using a computer! Aiden is helping me learn how to use it and a program called Word. You can type letters and all sorts of things in it. It even checks your spelling too. Now you will be able to read my letters without any problems.

I am seeing Dr. Maynard once a week. He is helping me understand and cope with my life with Mud. Dr. Maynard says coping is how a person handles something. I am learning how to handle my emotions when I think about Mud. It is hard because even though he hurt me, I still love him. He will always be my brother.

Charlene is taking good care of me. She likes to cook but she is letting me teach her some of my cooking show recipes. And Ruth gave me a job at Toad in the Hole. Sometimes I take orders and sometimes I help Merle in the kitchen. The people of Jubilee are very nice to me. I wish I had gotten to be a part of the community here a long time ago. But it is okay. I am a part of them now.

I miss you a lot. I am trying to teach Aiden how to play backgammon but I am not a very good teacher. He told me yesterday that he would look up how to play online. I think that is another computer thing. I hope he learns soon because I really want to play. I did teach him how to play Uno with doubles and triples and he likes that a lot. Sometimes Charlene plays with us.

If it's okay, I would really like to come visit you soon. Your house and your land sounded really wonderful when you told me about them. I will ask Aiden if he will drive me there, but only if it is okay with you.

How are you doing? I hope you are seeing your doctor, too. It is very helpful.

Please write back. I would like to hear from you soon.

Love,

Owen

"Oh, Owen. Looks like we both got a brand new Day One."

Acknowledgments

Thank you, first, to my amazing beta readers Laura, Valerie, Nikki, and Katie. Your feedback during the process of writing this book was invaluable. This story is a departure from my normal writing and you let me know that was okay. Thank you for being the first to fall in love with Caroline's story of strength and survival. I couldn't have made it through writing this very difficult story without you!

Thank you to the incredible team behind AnnaLisa Grant Books. Without the support of my amazing publicist Rick Miles at Red Coat PR, and my phenomenal agent Italia Gandolfo at GHF Literary, I may have thrown in the towel ages ago. Your encouragement and belief in my work in worth more than you know. Thank you for all you do!

To Marisa Shor at Cover Me, Darling, thank you for this gorgeous cover! Thank you for listening and creating a cover that begins to tell this story so well. You are a creative mastermind and I adore you!

Thank you to my awesome editor, Jessica at Rare Bird Editing. This was a difficult story and you did an amazing job at keeping the focus on the strength of the words and characters. Not only did you fix all my editing issues, but I also have you to thank for my Orphan Black addiction!

And to my formatter extraordinaire, Sharon at Amber Leaf Publishing, thank you for saving me from what has only amounted to a severe headache and lots of cursing. I'm grateful for your skills that get my work through all the meat grinders!

And to my girls Michele G. Miller and Samantha Davis: thank you for being sounding boards and writing partners. I am so grateful for your friendship!

I continue to be blown away on a daily basis by the unconditional love and support from my husband and children. We are closing in on six years of this adventure and not once have you batted an eye at my crazy writing schedule or the wild ideas that come out of my brain. This journey would mean nothing if I didn't have you by my side. Thank you for loving me!

Finally, to every woman who has ever been the victim of any form of sexual assault. Your stories of survival have impacted me in ways you may never comprehend. I am inspired by your strength, your tenacity, and your determination to not let your assault define you. You are amazing.

If you've been the victim of sexual assault, please don't hesitate to reach out for help.

You are strong. You are a survivor.

Rape, Abuse, & Incest National Network
www.rainn.org / 800-656-HOPE

Also by AnnaLisa Grant

<u>The Lake Series</u>

The Lake
Troubled Waters
Safe Harbor
Anchored

FIVE

As I Am

Oxblood
(Available 9/20/2016)

99 Days

AnnaLisa Grant

Made in the USA
Lexington, KY
22 May 2017